Something Magical

Leighann Dobbs

with Emely Chase

This is a work of fiction.

None of it is real. All names, places, and events are products of the author's imagination. Any resemblance to real names, places, or events are purely coincidental, and should not be construed as being real.

SOMETHING MAGICAL
Copyright © 2016
Leighann Dobbs
All Rights Reserved.

No part of this work may be used or reproduced in any manner, except as allowable under "fair use," without the express written permission of the author.

Something Magical

Chapter One

Esmerelda Seville's early morning humming lilted softly through the chilly stillness inside the old, three story building that housed the antique shop on the corner of Hawthorne and 7th Street, the sound filling the room with a whimsical air as she slowly made her way among the various rows of shelving, her wandering gaze carefully inspecting each item in turn.

As one of the three co-owners of *Seville's Antiques and Collectibles*, it was her job to make sure the polished wooden shelves inside the store always appeared to be fully stocked and today they were brimming with brilliant artwork, unique handicrafts, priceless knickknacks, and lots of high quality vintage pieces—both exotic and mundane—from all over the world.

But it was not the harmless little glamour spell she had cast that Esmerelda was checking this morning. Instead, she was searching for the special bits; pieces which remained *outside* the enchantment. Specific items with specific purposes; tokens which would allow her and her sisters to complete their latest assignment.

Having already checked every inch of every shelf in the wide open room once, she was just beginning her second pass when a glistening reflection from something in her periphery caught her eye. Excited now, she hurried over to a section of shelving near the back wall and lifted a shimmering, water-filled glass ball from its base, turning it this way and that to stir up the contents inside.

Watching as artificial snow spilled down, cascading over a lovely winter scene, Esmerelda called out to her sisters, her voice easily carrying from the main chamber on the lower floor to the small back room office next door. "What a pretty snow globe! Did you two know we had this back here?"

Enthralled, she turned the fragile glass in her hands again, shaking it slightly this time. She smiled when the falling snow inside settled softly along the curving boughs of several tall evergreens and blanketed the roof before gently coming to rest upon the ground around a lovely house which had been painted a soft, powder blue.

It wasn't a large house but there was something about the compact, two-story miniature structure that made it seem cozy. It was *quaint*, Esmerelda thought. Simple, and yet comfortable. The kind of house in which a family might live. A handsome, strong man, perhaps, who wasn't afraid of things which were different, and an adoring wife who worshiped him.

Allowing her thoughts to wander and the fantasy she had conjured in her mind to continue, she pictured an adventurous little boy with green eyes like his father, an adorable little blue-eyed girl who looked just like her mother, and maybe even a dog, she decided.

It was the type of house she herself might like to live in someday, Esmerelda thought wistfully. *Home.*

Banishing the fantasy that was beginning to play out in her thoughts with a quick shake of her head before one of her sisters picked up on it, she continued to stare almost trance-like into the glass, taking careful note of the startlingly vivid detail worked into each item inside the ball.

The quaint but cozy two-story house and its snow-covered lawn was surrounded on three sides by a white, intricately worked lattice fence which was covered by the thick and twisted empty vines of several climbing rose bushes.

A stone-edged graveled walk made a relatively straight path from a side door to the gated opening in the fence, its lines marred only by the junction of a second walkway leading to the front of the house. A tiny, white painted mailbox perched just outside the gate and the thick black lines of the house number stood out in stark relief against the bright white of the mailbox: *214.*

"Hey, two fourteen," she called casually over her shoulder to her sisters, her gaze still locked on the scene within the glass, but Serephina and

Mortianna were too busy chattering among themselves about the depression glass the lady who was coming by this morning would be looking for to hear her.

"She's looking for a *green* piece, Feeny," Esmerelda heard Mortianna tell her sister. "Green! We have exactly *one*. All the others are amber and rose—and *none* of them have our numbers. Can't we just whip one up? I mean, it's not like she'll know magic was involved. Nobody does. People don't believe in it anymore."

And it was that simple truth which had allowed the sisters to settle into Hawthorne Grove almost thirty years ago. Well, that and their *assignments*.

The numbers Mortianna had mentioned just happened to be the girls' date of birth, and its presence on any of the antiquities in their shop actually meant something—something very specific—but only to them. If an item had the Seville numbers on it, whether painted on or molded in or even carved inside, the girls knew it was the designated piece to be infused with their special brand of magic—one that would ensure the proper results for their assignments.

"No, we cannot *whip one up*, Morty," Serephina scolded. "And you keep your naughty little fingers to yourself because you know that's not true. Remember the Dover girl two summers back? *She* believed in magic *and* she knew the afghan we sold her was enchanted. Lucky for us, she didn't figure out we were the ones who spelled it in the first place. We almost got caught and it was *your* fault."

Esmerelda remembered that afghan. It was mauve and pastel pink, crocheted in a hounds tooth pattern. The girls had infused it so that whenever the Dover girl lay beneath it, she would think of her predestined mate. Feeny had given the infusion a little "extra" charge, however, and the lady knew there was something not quite normal going on because her thoughts and feelings were far too strong in relation to whenever she wasn't wrapped in the afghan.

"Hello? Valentine's Day?" Esmerelda called to them again, this time from the doorway, but her sisters continued to ignore her. She sighed. One would think her having broken in on their argument not once but twice in as many minutes would have been enough to put a stop to their petty bickering, but *no*. Not Mortianna and Serephina. When those two got started it was practically impossible for anyone to get a word in edgewise.

"*My* fault?" Mortianna's eyes narrowed accusingly and she pointed a finger at her older sibling. "*You* were the one who gave her the fertility poem and told her to recite it!"

It was days like this that made Esmerelda wonder if being a Seville was even worth it. Did Hawthorne Grove really need them? Was their special brand of matchmaking magic even necessary to bring their lost lovers together? They had Valentine's Day, after all, and it should have been enough ... but she knew it wasn't. Sure, Cupid had his bow and arrows, but *he* only worked one day a year. The Seville girls worked all year round. When they weren't bickering among themselves about who was responsible for whatever mishaps had taken place over the years.

Holding out the glass between her hands like an offering, Esmerelda stepped between her sisters and said, "Ladies! Snow globe. 214. Valentine's Day. Ring any bells?"

"What? It doesn't snow on Valentine's Day, Merry," Mortianna grouched, barely paying attention, but when she finally glanced in Esmerelda's direction she seemed to realize there was something important in what her sister had said—something that she had missed. "Wait, what are you talking about?"

Now that she knew she had her sister's undivided attention, at last, Esmerelda said, "It's the house numbers, see?"

Slowly, she turned the globe in her hands so her sisters could look inside. "214. February the fourteenth. Our birthday. This is it!"

"Well, bring it here," Serephina insisted, motioning her forward with an impatient wave. "If it has our numbers inside, this must be the piece we need."

Mortianna's expression was doubtful. "A snow globe? She's looking for depression glass. *Green* depression glass, remember? *This* glass is clear as crystal and cold as ice inside. How in the world is something like that supposed to warm her up to the idea of trusting a man again?"

"*She* has a name," Esmerelda reminded her

sister and then motioned with a quick tilt of her head toward the front door of the shop. "It's Kaylee, remember? And unless my perfect eyesight fails me, I believe that's her standing out there on the sidewalk, trying to decide whether or not it is safe to come inside. Hurry up, Feeny! Do it now, before she gets to the door!"

* * *

Kaylee Dean glanced at her watch and then up at the dilapidated building in front of her before speaking into her cell phone, answering her cousin, who was waiting for her to confirm she had located the antique shop in Hawthorne Grove. "This place looks like it has seen better days, Min, but it says *Seville Antiques and Collectibles* right over the door so I guess this is it."

"That's the place, yes. Thanks, Kay. You're a doll for doing this for me. Mom will never guess!"

"You're welcome, Min. Talk to you in a bit," she said and then ended the connection. Sliding her phone into her back jeans pocket wasn't as easy this winter morning as it was in spring and summer. For one thing, she didn't wear anything as bulky as the ash gray and black trimmed pea coat currently belted at her middle in the warmer months. For another, she generally wasn't so distracted by the utter lack of modern *anything* when she visited a place of business.

Seville's Antiques and Collectibles looked like a run-down warehouse straight out of the mid-1900's or, as her cousin Mindy would say: so last century! No wonder Min wanted her to come here to look for the depression glass ... it was probably still being freshly made inside!

Kaylee had been told the shop held a vast array of priceless antiquities but she found that hard to believe when the building itself looked like it might fall over if you so much as sneezed beside it.

The two story frame boasted a cracked and badly weathered wooden exterior, nicked and worn hardwood doors—even the window frames were no more than thin bits of old wood—some of it worm-eaten—and panes of plain, clear glass gone cloudy with age.

Not to mention, Kaylee couldn't see a single shred of evidence the owners had taken any precaution whatsoever to secure the place from thieves and vandals. Didn't they know anyone could walk by and knock out a window—probably with no more effort than it would take to flick away a noisome fly? With such valuable pieces reportedly inside, how could they risk getting broken into? Granted, Hawthorne Grove was a smallish town but it had its share of bad apples, she was sure. Weren't the owners even a little bit worried about losing their priceless inventory?

"Maybe it's not so valuable after all," she muttered, having finally managed to stuff her phone into her pocket.

Three steps later, she was tugging at the heavy brass door handle, and then she stepped inside. Overhead, the loud jingle of bells caught her attention and she glanced wryly toward the ceiling, expecting to see a string of round, silver bells suspended from bare, maybe even broken rafters, but she was met instead with a view of the store's interior she certainly had not anticipated.

The main room was much larger than she had thought it would be; it spanned two full stories in height. In the ceiling, wooden beams were exposed, but they were neither worn nor rotting. Instead, they were thick and strong, their surfaces gleaming in the morning sunlight that spilled through the uncovered windows as if they had just been freshly polished. Unlike outside, the mullioned windows were neatly trimmed with more burnished wood, and she could see heavy, lustrous brass latches securing each one.

"Good morning! May we help you?" a voice called from the back of the store and she glanced around, moving instinctively through the tall rows of display shelves toward the sound of warm greeting while her eyes busily scanned the room in both surprise and awe.

"Hello. I am looking for depression glass and an acquaintance said I should check here ... " she explained, her words trailing off as her attention was caught by first one exquisite piece and then another.

Brow furrowed in confused astonishment, she turned, trying to absorb it all but she found the whole of her experience thus far almost too diametrically opposed to take in. The sheer beauty filling every nook and niche inside the shop, after having witnessed the results of what must have been many years of painful neglect on the outside, was almost ...

"Unbelievable," she whispered, her jaw slack as she was still held in a bit of a trance by her reaction to the surprise, but when a woman appeared from the back carrying some sort of glass object, she snapped her mouth shut and offered a nod of greeting.

"Isn't it?" the lady agreed in passing, and Kaylee felt her cheeks burn with embarrassment from having been overheard.

"We have some lovely Mayfair Pink pieces..." the woman said in reference to her explanation of what she was looking for.

"No, it must be green," Kaylee said. "It is for my aunt, you see. She has been collecting depression glass for a few years now and green is the color she is currently on about, so Min says it must be green."

Her words did not seem to trouble the woman at all. In fact, she seemed more concerned with carefully situating the glass object she had been carrying upon the front counter than she was with her customer at the moment, and Kaylee found herself growing inexplicably curious about the piece.

"As luck would have it, we do have the green, but there is only the one piece. I'm sure there will be more soon, but for now—" She held up the glass ball and shook it. Light sparkled through the cut glass, creating dozens of rainbow prisms which seemed to shoot out through the room in all directions. Then, she walked a few feet to the checkout counter and shifted a few bits and baubles to one side before removing something from her pocket, which she placed in the center of the counter. Next, she settled the glass carefully onto the thing—an intricately carved wooden stand, Kaylee realized—before finally stepping away with a look of happy satisfaction on her face.

"There!" she said, her expression positively radiating with glee. She squeezed her hands together in front of her chest and glanced up at Kaylee to ask, "Isn't it lovely?"

Kaylee wandered over as if she were being summoned, once more feeling inexplicably drawn to the thing, and when she looked inside the ball, she found it difficult to look away. A tiny blue house sat on a bed of snow, and the whole of the scene was surrounded by trees, a fence, and—there was even a tiny mailbox outside the gate at the edge of a snow-covered lane with no end and no beginning.

"Beautiful," she agreed, running her fingers lightly over the sparkling clear glass. Despite the cold scene inside, Kaylee felt a rush of warmth filling her, spreading from her gloved fingertips to her toes. She did not even lift her head to ask, "How much is it?"

"$225, but if you're buying the depression glass, I'll give it to you for half," the lady said, stepping quickly behind the counter. She bent down to rummage beneath, her hands emerging seconds later with one near mint condition piece of depression glass. "I think your aunt will love this one."

Five minutes later, Kaylee exited the store with her purchases carefully wrapped and bagged and a happy smile on her lips. Excited, she reached back to fish her cellphone out of her pocket and quickly flicked through with her thumb across the two screens it took to contact her cousin before raising it to her ear.

Mindy answered after only two rings.

"I got it, Min!" Kaylee said in a rush. "A Hazel-Atlas Royal Lace dinner plate. Green, yes. No visible flaws and it isn't sick, either! Twenty-five dollars, and Min? I bought something for myself, too. It is so beautiful. I can hardly wait for you to see it!"

Chapter Two

"Oh! My bad. My bad," Jordan Parker said, swiftly reaching out to steady the young woman he'd almost sent sprawling before she lost her balance completely. "I was so busy trying to figure out why anyone would recommend a place that looks like it's so old it's about to crumble into the dirt, I forgot to look where I was going."

"I know, right?" she said breathlessly once she was on surer footing, but he couldn't tell whether her breathlessness was from the biting chill of the frosty morning air or reaction to her near fall.

"But don't let the exterior fool you," she continued. "They have everything you could possibly imagine inside."

Jordan studied her, a bemused smile curling his lips. She was a short little bit of a thing. Petite, he guessed was more the correct term, and she was ... well ... *cute.* From the fuzzy little pink ball on the top of her soft knit pink cap to the glossy sheen of her black half-boots, everything about her said *peppy.* He caught himself wondering if spirited girls like her ever agreed to have coffee with sentimental idiots like himself. "Really? You'd never guess it from here."

"Oh, yes!" she insisted excitedly, her wide brown eyes sparkling with a warm glow he found it hard to look away from. Her hair, or what he could see of it where it poured from beneath her cap, was also brown—a rich, warm chestnut, gilt throughout with tendrils of fire—and her lips... "It's like a magic store in there!"

"Hello?"

The word was muted, as if it were coming from a great distance and he saw in the changing of her expression the moment the sound registered in her ears. Her eyes widened and she glanced away from him while hurriedly raising her cellphone to her ear. He listened in as she quickly began to apologize, "Sorry, Min! Sorry! I was—"

Her cheeks colored with what he supposed was embarrassment over having forgotten she'd been on a call, and again, he found himself bemused. Not by her, but at himself. His reaction to her. She was peppy and breathless and colored with a delightful blush and he was surprised to realize that he liked everything he saw.

Her shoulders rose and fell in a quick shrug as she angled the coral pink iPhone away from her soft pink lips to whisper, "Excuse me. I forgot my cousin was still on!"

Without really knowing why, he grinned. Wow, he thought. Everything about this girl was ... *warm* somehow. Her eyes, her hair, and now her cheeks.

He took a step closer, not even realizing he hadn't let go of her until she shrugged away from him and offered a quick half-smile of apology. "Thanks for saving me! I have to run, but I hope you find what you're looking for in there."

Jordan snatched his hands down to his sides, stepped sideways out of her path, and nodded. "Yep."

He couldn't seem to take his eyes off her, and as she hurried away, he caught a few words of her phone conversation.

"...going in as I was coming out. What? Oh. Yeah, he is, I suppose..." She glanced back over her shoulder at him and he smiled. She smiled back and then promptly forgot he existed as she turned to work the keys in her gloved palm to unlock her car.

Sentimental idiot for sure, Jordan admonished himself silently, shaking his head at the insane direction his thoughts had taken as he turned to enter the antique store. He'd just gotten out of a relationship. Now was definitely not the time to be thinking about asking someone he didn't even know to share a few hours of conversation over a cup of mocha crème latte with him at Sam's.

* * *

"*Why* did you throw them into one another like that?" Serephina bit out, scolding her sister in a heated whisper while continuing to watch the couple outside from behind the counter in the shop. "You *know* we aren't supposed to interfere!"

"And what do you call giving them magic-infused items that will bring the two of them together if not interference, hmm?" Mortianna shot back. "Besides, it's a dull, dead bore to watch them come in here and then leave like two ships passing in the night, the one never seeing the other until they are well out of our sight."

Her grumpy pout disappeared as quickly as it had appeared, the corner of her lips suddenly kicking up in a half-grin. "At least *this* way we get to see a little *action*! Did you two notice he never took his hands off her until she shrugged? No, wait. Did you notice *she* didn't realize he hadn't until her blasted cousin butted in? You *know* she was feeling it. Heck, *I* was feeling it—from all the way in here! Those smoldering gray eyes of his are sexy enough to make any woman's—"

"Mouth *shut*," Serephina commanded with a swift flick of her wrist, silencing Mortianna before her runaway tongue could do any more damage to the situation, then she turned to greet their latest customer with what she hoped was a warm smile as the bells over the door jangled out a noisy warning. "Good morning, sir!"

Sliding off his dark sunglasses, he slowly folded them and slid them into the inside pocket of his heavy charcoal gray bomber jacket, his gaze roaming over the front interior of the store before he nodded to each of the sisters in turn. "Ladies."

"Can we help you find something?" Serephina asked, surreptitiously motioning for Mortianna to bring the box around, but Esmerelda swept it out of her hands.

"I'll just put this in the back," she said, making sure to pass by him on her way. His eyes flickered to it as she passed and his hand shot out, halting her.

"Hold on. Is that mahogany?"

"Mm hmm," Esmerelda murmured. "It's a bit worn, but look at this. Metal string work, inlaid Mother Of Pearl..."

She turned the box, tilting it a bit so he could see it better, but he reached for it instead. "Do you mind if I have a closer look?"

Smiling, she handed it over to him. "Not at all. It really is a lovely box. English, I believe, but I'm not quite sure what these hooks on the sides are for... "

"A pen, or quill, and a letter opener," he offered without further encouragement.

"There's a bit of the spiral trim work missing up here, and the feet—see, you can tell where they once were—" he said, pointing out the rounded indentations on the box's bottom, "are missing."

"Yes, I see. You are very astute. It does have a few flaws. The missing feet, a bit of string work, trim, and the inside is a bit picky though intact."

"There are numbers here, too. Likely the mark of the creator. See? They've been carved into the wood on the bottom. Looks like 2-1-4."

"Numbered? Well, then, that makes it even more rare and wonderful! Serephina, this one is marked, darling. Remember the Avrochelle set from last year? This box must be the second item in a single desk set made up of four pieces. Should I put it in the other room until we've located the others?" She peered over her shoulder at her sister, who bit at her lip to erase the growing smile that tried to appear at his words.

"Oh, my, yes! The set will bring much more. We can't—"

"I'll give you two fifty for it," he said. "I know it's worth less—I'm a bit of a hobbyist collector myself—but I'm willing to lose a little to bring it home today."

Esmerelda frowned. "Oh, I don't know. We would actually prefer to find the other pieces. This one is clearly part of a set, you see. If it is like the Avrochelle set, there would be a blotter, an ink stand, and an—"

"Oh, of course we will give it to him, Merry," Serephina called out. "Would you like it wrapped, sir?"

With barely a glance at Esmerelda, he walked over to the counter, placed the box carefully to one side and took out his wallet. "Thank you, ma'am, but it isn't a gift."

"Ah, I see," Serephina said. She picked up the box and placed it inside a paperboard box before sliding both into a thick, gray craft paper bag.

"I saw you with the lady outside and I thought— oh, well, it doesn't really matter what I think." Waving away her words as if she were embarrassed to have made such a guess, she said, "We'll take one eighty."

He nodded and placed a few bills on the counter

along with a business card. He tapped it, and picked up the box. "If you happen to locate the other pieces, give me a call. Thank you, ladies."

"No, thank *you*," Esmerelda said as he made his way to the door. The minute he stepped outside the shop, she turned to her sisters with a wide-eyed look of awe. "Did you see those *eyes*? Oh my! Miss Dean isn't going to know what hit her!"

* * *

At home, Jordan tossed the local paper onto one side of his kitchen table and set the package containing the letter box on the other. The overhead lighting in here was much better for allowing him to inspect it properly and as he lifted it out of the bag he looked at each side, his fingertips running along the edges of the inlaid mother-of-pearl while his brain made notes of the various repairs he'd need to do. New legs, a short length of mahogany for repairing the chip on the front. With just a bit of refinishing, the box would almost be like new.

Jordan was fully aware most collectors preferred to find pieces in pristine original condition, but he rather enjoyed restoring those he found that were in such poor condition nobody wanted them. There was a certain satisfaction in taking something worn and broken and making it whole again.

He himself had amassed a nice collection of letter boxes like this one over the years, but he wasn't in it for the money, so the fact that restoration tended to make a piece less valuable than an untouched original didn't bother him. Reclaiming antique boxes was a surprising pasttime he'd stumbled upon and it was work he loved to lose himself in.

Cautiously, he opened the box. The hinges still worked, but the pale blue paper lining that had been glued to the interior over a hundred years ago was picked and beginning to peel in spots. One corner was worse than the rest, and ... he squinted at the paper. It looked like something had been wedged between the paper and the side of the box.

Turning, he rummaged through a drawer until he found a pair of tweezers, which he used to pick gently at the item beneath the loosened paper, he pushed it slightly forward, hoping to move it along the edge until he could finally get a hold on it.

Whatever the thing was, it was thin. He didn't want to damage the box but his curiosity was piqued. Using the end of the tweezers, he painstakingly inched the mysterious item hidden inside the box toward a tear in the corner. The thing was a devil to move beneath the tightly glued paper—until it reached that last, crucial centimeter. He almost had it out without mishap, but then his hand slipped and the blasted thing popped free. Without warning, it jumped the edge of the box, and pinged off his marbled counter top before landing on the unread paper he'd tossed on the kitchen table earlier—right over a notice from the local animal rescue shelter.

Afraid he'd irreparably marred the interior of the box, Jordan ignored it to inspect the damage, but miraculously, the thing had sprung free without leaving a scratch ... on the box. *He* was the one who had taken damage from that little battle. In his struggle to keep the box from sliding off the table while trying to catch whatever had sprung free at the same time, he'd sustained a nasty scratch on his inner forearm from the tweezers. He barely gave it a glance, though, because once he was satisfied the box hadn't been damaged, he'd sat it aside and reached for the thing lying on top of the paper to see what had been hidden inside.

It was some sort of metallic, oval tag—brass, he decided once he saw the murky green patina creeping around its edges. Picking it up, he held the thing closer to the light, and realized almost immediately what it was—a license tag from a dog's collar. An image of Royal—the golden retriever who had been with him since high school —sprang to mind. He rubbed the tag lightly between his finger and thumb, his thoughts drifting back to the last time he'd held a license like this: it was just after Royal had died two years ago while he was out of town on business.

Stacy, his girlfriend at the time, hadn't even bothered to call him, to let him know Royal was sick. To give her a bit of credit, she *had* finally taken the retriever to the vet after he'd explained what she needed to do, but it was too little, too late. Royal had been too far gone at that point to save.

"It's just a dog, Jordan," she had told him when he'd explained she needed to get him to the animal hospital as quickly as possible.

He'd felt alarmed and amazed by her attitude, but now he knew Stacy would never understand the bond between a man and his dog—just as she'd never understood his affinity for antique letter boxes. She had called them both a waste of his time and money.

Maybe she was right about part of it, he grudgingly admitted. He did have a rather large collection of antique boxes sitting empty throughout the house and today he'd still been stoked to find yet another to add to his collection. At this point, even *he* didn't understand why he kept buying them when he couldn't find anything to do with the ones he already had. Maybe he kept buying them because he was secretly hoping to find something worth keeping?

Not that the why mattered. Stacy would never have approved. How many times had she snapped at him for buying "more old junk" when he clearly had no use for the junk he already had? She'd pretended concern, telling him it seriously frightened her that he could not see how he was wasting his money—but she'd had no problem wasting it for him. It had been *his* credit card she'd used to pay for her three-month trip to the Caribbean, and *his* bank account that had covered the cost of the brand new Mercedes she was driving the day he'd finally had enough and ordered her to pack up her stuff and get out.

Jordan rubbed the tag between his thumb and fore-finger once more, pushing away the unwanted memories of his ex-girlfriend and the pain of his loss over the loyal retriever he so badly missed.

His eyes fell on the paper. It was showing an ad for the *Cressley Cade Animal Rescue Society*. There was a picture of a Golden Retriever that reminded him of Royal and who was apparently up for adoption right now. Jordan glanced back at the tag he was holding and the beginnings of a smile curved his lips.

Now that he was settled in his new home and had all the time in the world to do whatever he wanted, he'd realized it wasn't enough. Things were far too quiet here with him alone and he knew he wasn't ready to begin a new relationship, but a dog—yes, a dog was exactly what he needed.

Scooping up the paper, he quickly typed the address of the Animal Rescue Society into the navigational app on his phone. Then, he stuck the dog tag in his pocket, picked up the box, and headed for the door.

Chapter Three

Kaylee knelt down beside the new mother chihuahua and her litter of three.

"She really is the sweetest thing, Mrs. Conrad, and such a good mama," she said to the elderly lady at her side before running her hand down the mother chihuahua's back. With her index finger, she gently nussed the mother dog under her chin before smoothing her palm down her back again. "Aren't you, Mimi? Aren't you? Such a good girl! Yes, you are!"

To the lady, she said, "The pups were born three days ago, so she won't be going anywhere for a few weeks. But once the little ones are weaned, we would be happy to give you a call."

Even as she said the words, Kaylee felt a wave of sadness for the wee pups. After three years of working at the *Cressley Cade Animal Rescue Society*, she still could not make herself be the one responsible for separating a litter from its mother. She would not be the one making this call, either.

She didn't exactly know why, but in all this

time, she still couldn't make herself do it. Separation anxiety was what her sister Jo called it. Jo had even gone so far as to suggest Kaylee's being jilted one month before her wedding was the most likely cause for it, but Kaylee didn't think so. She just could not bear the thought of the pups being separated from their mother, or vice-verse. It kept her up at night—much like the man from the antique store, she realized, a frown pulling at her brow.

"Would it be okay for me to complete the paperwork now, Miss Dean?" the gray-haired lady who had introduced herself as Mrs. Conrad asked.

Pushing away the cheerless gloom she'd slipped into, Kaylee covered her involuntary shudder behind the act of rising to her feet. Miraculously, she remembered to smile. "Of course. If you'll just speak with Marc over there, he will make sure everything's taken care of."

"Excuse me, Miss. Can you help me?" There was a rattle of paper behind her left shoulder and Kaylee realized the man to whom the voice belonged was talking to *her*.

"There was a dog in Sunday's paper—a golden retriever who had been hit by a truck and then abandoned? I was hoping to give him a new home," the oddly familiar voice continued. "Is he still here?"

"That would be Sarge, and he is right outsi—" Kaylee paused in the act of turning, and froze. It was *him*—the man from the antique shop. The man who'd kept her up every night since they'd met outside that store more than a week ago.

Today, he wasn't wearing the dark shades he'd had on before, and her first look into his smoky gray eyes was nothing short of mesmerizing. She saw within them the spark of recognition when he realized who she was and tried to look away, but she could not.

"Well, hello again," he said with a smile, his tone making it clear he had recognized her, too, and Kaylee fought to find her tongue.

"You go ahead and help this young man, dear," Mrs. Carson said, giving Kaylee's shoulder an understanding pat as she moved away. "I'll just speak with Marc."

As Mrs. Carson walked away, the man with the startling gray eyes offered her his hand. "Since we keep meeting up, I suppose I should introduce myself. I'm Jordan Parker."

"Kaylee," she said, hesitantly placing her palm in his. "Kaylee Dean."

Something in his eyes changed, but she wasn't sure what. "It is a pleasure to meet you, Miss Dean."

The feel of his bare palm sliding against hers was electrifying. A surge of heat raced up her arm, making her entire body tingle with awareness—unsettling awareness. Quickly, she pulled her hand away to rub it consolingly against her other palm. Clearing her throat to force the words past the knot of anxiety she could feel forming there, she said, "If you will follow me, Mr. Parker."

Break eye contact, she told herself. *Now turn, and*

walk. Her body followed her mental instructions but her mind tangled around some very disturbing realizations. He smelled like a teddy bear. Not the mundane, textile scent of fibers and thread and poly-fill, but rather, the surprisingly comforting aroma of cuddly, warm male mixed with a hint of mystery and an exciting though forbidden top note of yum. Kaylee felt a sudden urge to curl up around him and sigh.

Stop it, Kaylee, she demanded. *A secure haven in which to snuggle up and lose yourself forever? Really? He's just a man, for Pete's sake! And a stranger, at that!*

"Jordan," he insisted, falling into step behind her, and Kaylee experienced a second of fright in which she was terrified he'd been able to read her thoughts.

"Have you owned a pet before, Mr. Parker?" she finally asked, trying to break through her own sudden feelings of awkwardness with seemingly related bits of conversation.

"Royal," he said. "Also a golden retriever. I lost him two years ago. And you? Do you have a pet at home, Miss Dean?"

Her thoughts were instantly filled with visions of being met at her door by *him*, in a towel, and of herself immediately dropping her purse to run her eager hands all over him.

What in the world is wrong with you? He means a dog, she cautioned her wayward thoughts. *Or a cat. Or any domesticated animal but definitely not a man, so stop it already!* But she could not stop the burning flush she felt spreading upward from her neck. She shook her head. "No, I don't."

Flustered and annoyed because of it, she practically raced ahead of him to the outdoor kennels. Reaching the larger one Ms. Cade had assigned to Sarge, she reached out to flip the latch and open the door.

"This is Sarge, Mr. Parker." Snapping her fingers, she whistled for the golden retriever whose ears had perked up the instant she touched the latch. "Sarge? Here boy. Come on out and say hello."

To her surprise, Jordan Parker squatted, putting himself on eye level with the rehabilitated retriever, held out his hand, and then waited for the dog to come to him. It took a moment, but the dog finally ambled cautiously out of the pen to sniff at his outstretched hand. A few seconds later, his tongue was lolling and his tail happily wagging.

"Hiya Sarge. How are you doing, boy? Enjoying yourself here, are you?" Mr. Parker asked as he reached out to ruffle the dog's fur, first behind his head and then beneath his chin. He leaned closer, tilting his head to the side as if to hear whatever Sarge's answer to his questions had been, and said, "Oh, I know. I think so, too. In fact, I was just about to."

Turning on his haunches, the man looked up at Kaylee, offering a hesitant, almost shy smile that made her knees turn to gelatin and said, "How about it, Miss Dean? Do you think you'd like to try the best mocha crème latte this side of the city?"

Kaylee's brow rose sharply at his back-handed

attempt to ask her out for coffee. "I don't think so."

Turning back to Sarge, he shrugged and said, "Hey, I tried, old man, but you heard the lady."

Despite her best intentions, Kaylee laughed. "What did he say?"

Jordan looked up at her, one brow arched. "That you are a very beautiful lady and I should probably ask you out, of course."

She rolled her eyes, ignoring the warmth shooting through her at his pretended second-hand compliment. "Sure he did."

"He also said he wanted to come home with me today but that *you* would insist I fill out a handful of papers first. Is this true, Miss Dean?" he asked, getting to his feet.

There was a hint of apology in his eyes when he glanced her way again and she wondered what it meant. Was he sorry he had asked her for a date? Inexplicably hurt by the thought, Kaylee nodded. "Yes, there are a few papers we would need you to complete, for our records."

"Well, there you have it," he said. Pushing his hands into the front pockets of his jeans, he rocked slightly on his feet and looked at the ground, motioning toward the dog with his elbow. "If old Sarge here didn't lie about the papers, why would he lie about you?"

There was sincerity in his questioning gaze this time when he looked at her, and Kaylee bit her lip, fighting an unexpected urge to reassure him—of what, she didn't know. Her brow furrowed and she turned away before she did something stupid. Like hug him.

"If you're serious about adopting Sarge, Mr. Parker, you can do the paperwork now. It'll be a few days before you can take him home, but—"

"I am absolutely serious about it, Miss Dean. As serious as I was about coffee. Are you sure you won't join me?"

* * *

Jordan Parker was no stranger to rejection. The first six investors he had approached about financing his fledgling IT business nine years ago had turned him down, too. Granted, he was only nineteen at the time, with very little experience to back up his business plan, but the numbers were right, and as it turned out, so was he.

Investor number seven had helped him prove it to the world.

Within five years, his company ranked in the top one hundred IT companies in the world. When he'd sold it off last year after he'd decided to retire, it was ranked number seven in the Fortune 500. But being turned down for coffee by the peppy Miss Dean was a rejection that felt *personal*.

Not that it should have. If he counted every minute since their first meeting until she walked away from him at the end of their last, they'd spent a total of eighteen minutes together—hardly enough time for him to turn her refusal to share his caffeine addiction into a personal jab—and yet, it had wounded him somehow. Not unlike the antique letter box he'd picked up last weekend at the antique shop, he thought, rubbing at his injured arm, but even that hadn't bothered him as much as this woman's whole I-don't-want-to-get-coffee-with-you thing, and he didn't know why.

It's probably just that over-inflated ego of yours, his conscience pricked as he followed her with his gaze. *She put a pin in it and the pain you feel is the effect of it slowly shrinking down to size.*

She hadn't waited around for him to finish the paperwork, either. After depositing him at one of the tables with a hasty mumble about someone being there to help him soon, she'd hurried off to see to another customer while he busied himself with watching her from afar as he made sure to dot all his "I's" and cross every "T".

Shifting in the chair, he reached into his pocket to collect the dog license he'd unearthed from the letter box and held it up to the light, trying to make out something other than the name. He could clearly read the series of numbers, but rest of it was far too corroded to read. Still, it *was* responsible for his being here today. He'd come to the shelter to adopt a dog—not pick up a woman, he reminded himself.

Slipping the warm metal tag back into his pocket, Jordan signed his name on the last sheet of paper and walked to the front desk where he laid both the pen and clip board aside. "I've filled in the important bits, my cell number and my signature. If you need anything else, give me a call."

Half an hour later, he was standing in his garage staring down in aggravated confusion at the antique letter box he'd moved to the worktable for dis-assembly. As he scowled down at it like it was some strangely intricate, impossibly difficult puzzle to be solved, he contemplated the ill-considered invitation he'd issued to Miss Dean to join him for coffee and then complained to the box that it was "just like a woman."

And by that, he meant confusing. Not knowing the reason for disappointment at being turned down by the woman from the antique shop was as irritating as not knowing where his illogical passion for buying antique letter boxes came from. At the moment, both currently posed a mystery for him that was gnawing at his insides and adding equally to his growing surly mood until, glaring down at the box, he reached over and slammed the lid firmly shut.

Why *did* he keep buying the darn things, anyway?

* * *

Huntingdon's One Shot Coffee Cafe was a cozy little coffee shop located on the outskirts of town to which quite a lot of Hawthorne Grove's residents gravitated, both in the mornings, for that first steaming cup of brew that the owner guaranteed would knock the sleep out of their eyes, and in the evenings when the lighting was dim, the mugs were thinner, and the exquisite brew topping every cup became a lot more artistic than the caffeinated jolt Sam Huntingdon faithfully served his sleepy-eyed customers in the A.M..

Jo Dean Leavy was a regular. In the four years during which the cafe had been in operation, she hadn't once missed a morning of stopping in for what she called her "emergency wake up call." But tonight, she was sitting at a ruby cloth-draped table, sipping a mocha crème latte for a different reason.

"Are you sure this whole lack of sleep thing is about Daniel? I mean, come on, Kaylee. It's been two years. You're concerned he's making you lose sleep again, but I know you. You're not the type to let a guy make you tuck tail and run—or hide," she told her sister. "Besides, dreaming about him doesn't necessarily mean you're thinking about or worrying about *him* in particular. Maybe your dreams are trying to tell you it's time you moved on. Time you let yourself find a man, and get into a relationship again. Have some fun for a change!"

She sat her cup on the table, leaned back in her chair, and looked her sister straight in the eye. Then, her eyes narrowed. "Oh, my God. That's it, isn't it? There's a *guy*! You've met someone who makes you think about getting serious again, and ... Kaylee Dean, you've been holding out on me, haven't you?"

Lifting the steaming cup to her lips, Kaylee almost felt guilty.

"There's no guy," she said, but she could feel the heat of a blush stealing its way up her neck to her cheeks. "I mean, there was a guy. I ran into him. Or, rather, he ran into me. But that's not important. It's just—coincidence."

Her sister was still peering at her through narrowed eyelids. "What coincidence?" Kaylee shrugged. "Remember last weekend when I promised Mindy I'd go to the antique place for her?"

Jo nodded. "The snow globe place? Yeah, you told me about it. Or I thought you had, but obviously you left out all the important bits."

There was a not-so-subtle hint of accusation in her tone that made Kaylee want to wince.

"No, I didn't. Having a guy in a dark gray bomber jacket almost run me over on the sidewalk was nothing. It was—" she shrugged. "It was just one of those things. But then he showed up at the shelter, and—"

"And you freaked," her sister filled in for her.

"I did *not* freak." Feeling defensive now, Kaylee broke eye contact and squirmed uncomfortably in her seat.

"I just ... turned him down. For coffee. Which *we* are having now," she said, lifting her cup once more.

Jo's eyebrows shot upward. "He asked you out? Wait a minute."

Leaning forward, she took Kaylee's cup from her and sat it aside before taking both her sister's hands in her own. "Let me make sure I get this straight. A guy almost knocks you off your feet at the antique shop, then he shows up at the shelter and asks you out. And you said no."

Kaylee nodded, but her sister clearly did not understand.

"Why? Was he butt-ugly or something?"

"No." Kaylee felt her nose crinkle, adding strength to her denial, and dropped back in her chair with a sigh. "He was actually quite handsome, especially after ... "

Realizing that she was about to reveal she had noticed a lot more about the guy than she cared to admit, Kaylee broke off with a shrug. "He looked decent enough, Jo. But he has nothing to do with my having gotten a total of four hours sleep every night since the day we ran into each other at Seville's."

"But what if he does?" Jo suggested, giving her fingers a little squeeze of encouragement. "What if you met this guy and your subconscious realized you liked him? What if, deep down, you wondered if it was okay to have a man in your life again, okay to trust a man again, and your dreams are just an extension of that, hmm?"

"What if it remembered what happened last time and dredged up scenarios from my past to present to me in my sleep as a warning against it?" Kaylee offered wryly, pulling her fingers out of her sister's grasp.

Jo's head dropped back and she closed her eyes. When she raised her head again, it was to glare in annoyance at her sister. "You're impossible sometimes, you know?"

"Mmm," Kaylee mumbled in agreement around

her last swallow of coffee. "And sleepy. I think it's time I headed home. Thanks for the latte, Jo, and the chat. Next time, I'll buy."

Jo fumbled in her purse for her credit card. "And maybe next time you'll listen to what I'm trying to tell you."

The bells over the coffee shop door rang out, drawing their attention as well as the owners, who was busily wiping down the bar counter with a damp cloth. "Hey, man! You made it!"

He walked around the bar and met the new customer half- way. The two embraced for a second, one of those back-slapping, guy things, and then the newcomer said, "Sammy! It's good to see you again. How's business?"

Kaylee felt a tingle of awareness at the sound of his voice, but she had known it was him the moment he stepped inside the cafe. Hoping to avoid notice, she dropped her eyes and tucked her chin. "See you tomorrow, Jo."

Half an hour later, still restless although she felt so tired she could barely hold her head up, Kaylee tied her bath robe and padded barefoot through the living room of her one bedroom apartment, making a bee-line for the snow globe. She still didn't know why she felt so drawn to the thing, but looking at it made her feel at ease somehow. Less troubled and less ... alone. Everything seemed so perfect inside. So peaceful and serene and ... .

Looking into the glass, she couldn't help but think the people in *that* house loved each other. Real love. The kind of love that didn't go away, ever, no matter what. The man inside would never walk out on his woman a month before their wedding, leaving her scarred and afraid to risk her heart again no matter how tempting it may be to do so.

Lifting the ball, she peered in at the beautiful abundance of thick, glistening snow covering the fence, the yard, the trees, the house, and Jo's words at the coffee shop came back to her. Was she finally getting over the pain of being jilted two years ago? Was she truly ready to start over, to try again for love?

Frowning now, she closed her eyes and shook the ball, thinking if her subconscious were really as smart as Jo seemed to think it was, it could have produced a much better sign or clue than torturing her from sleep with dreams of Daniel every night.

Give me a sign. The thought whispered unconsciously through her thoughts in the brief instant before she opened her eyes and looked down at the ball again. The snow, which moments before had blanketed every surface inside was in the air, was trickling slowly downward. But what caught her eye was the dog resting on his haunches on the path leading from the stoop outside the front door.

It looked a lot like Sarge, she thought. Definitely a golden retriever, but—how had she missed it before? Tilting the ball this way and that, she watched as artificial snow slowly covered the ground and walkway again, piling up over and around the dog while her thoughts drifted to a pair of fascinating gray eyes.

Setting the glass ball carefully back into its stand, she clicked off the lamp and headed into the bedroom. Slipping off her robe, she got into bed and pulled the quilt up to her chin. Staring unseeing through the darkness at the ceiling, she wondered if maybe Jo was right. Perhaps it *was* time she stopped letting what happened to her in the past keep her from enjoying the present.

Chapter Four

Kaylee woke the next morning feeling rested and strangely exhilarated. For the first time in a week, her sleep hadn't been interrupted by disturbing dreams of her ex-fiance; she'd actually slept the entire night through!

Still groggy, she stretched and turned to peer sleepily at her clock, wondering how long she had to laze in bed before her alarm went off. 8:00. Eight? No, that couldn't be right. She'd scheduled today's first grooming appointment for eight! Kaylee blinked once, then jolted into action. Springing up, she flung off the covers and grabbed her cell phone, quickly flipping through a few screens before punching the green call button with her thumb.

Her 8:00 a.m. appointment answered on the second ring. "Mrs. O'Reilly? Yes, it's Kaylee. I'm running a little late this morning, but I'm on my way. Can you give me fifteen minutes, or do we need to reschedule?"

"Fifteen minutes is fine," Mrs. O'Reilly said. "Is

there anything wrong, dear?"

After assuring Mrs. O nothing was wrong and embarrassingly admitting she'd just overslept— something quite unusual for her—Kaylee ended the call, rushed to the closet to gather a handful of clothes, and then locked herself in the bathroom for the quickest shower by a female, ever, and that rush seemed to set the tone of her day.

After her shower, she'd grabbed a banana and a granola bar from the kitchen and ate them both while getting dressed, and although she'd shamefully bent a few speeding laws in order to pull it off, somehow managed to make it to her shop, Kaylee's Pet Care and Grooming, with three minutes to spare before the fifteen she'd promised Mrs. O ran out.

Breathless from having run across half a parking lot and then up a flight of stairs, Kaylee used the time it took her to unlock and get inside her normal place of business to apologize again to Mrs. O for being late, and although Mrs. O'Reilly assured her it was no problem, Kaylee still only charged her half price for Mitzi's grooming to make up for her inexcusable tardiness.

The door had barely closed behind them when the phone rang. An emergency pet-icure, which she agreed to do in half an hour if they could make it in that short a time, then there were two walk-ins, plus her three regular Monday clients, and a bad delivery she'd had to send back to the supplier because half her order was missing and the other half was wrong—and it seemed like everyone in the county decided to call in after that to book a grooming for their pets. But when Marc called from the shelter at a little after two, Kaylee was still surprised to realize so much of the day was already gone.

"You okay? It's a quarter after two."

Kaylee waved goodbye to her last client for the day and sat down in her chair behind her desk. With a swoop of her hand, she pushed a bit of hair that had come loose from her hastily banded pony-tail out of her eyes and blew out a slow breath. "I'm sorry, Marc. Today has been a special kind of crazy."

"Yeah? Well, you can tell me about it when you get here. Daina had to leave early and Ren never showed, so step on it, lady. I need all the help I can get over here and you're already late."

And so, for the second time that day, Kaylee grabbed her purse and her keys, locked the door, and rushed to her car to hurry to an appointment at which she should already have arrived.

By five thirty, she was more than ready for a break ... a long one.

"Whew. It's been hectic today," Marc said. He brought a folder to the table and dropped it in front of her. "Almost closing time, and I have to admit, I am definitely looking forward to it."

Kaylee flipped open the folder. "What's this?"

"Mr. Parker's paperwork. Everything's in order. He can pick up the retriever whenever he's ready." He walked away from the table, stopping at the door to collect his jacket. "I was hoping you'd call him before you leave. I've got a date I'd hate to be late for. It's a first, and you know how picky you ladies are about things like that."

He didn't wait for her answer. Instead, he shrugged on his jacket and, smiling back at her over his shoulder as he stepped through the door, waved a jaunty goodbye. "See you tomorrow, Kaylee Bean!"

Only he wouldn't, Kaylee thought a bit grumpily, because she wouldn't be there. She volunteered at the shelter three days a week—something he had forgotten in his rush to meet his latest *first* date—and Tuesdays weren't one of those three days.

In front of her, the paperwork for Sarge's adoption taunted and she closed the folder. Did she really want to put herself through seeing Jordan Parker again? She'd been so busy today she hadn't thought of him even once. But now, she clearly remembered the last time she'd seen him, she'd lost a week of sleep—and he'd only asked her out to coffee!

Then again, she hadn't thought of Daniel either, and that realization was shocking because she knew she had angsted at least once every single day of the past two years over his unexpected defection. The shock of Daniel's calling off their wedding had quite nearly paralyzed her. The mere thought of putting herself in a similar position for pain again almost made her physically ill.

But there was something about Jordan Parker, something in his eyes that called to her. Something in the way he'd looked at her—half confident, half mortified—that made her think she might be okay with him. Long enough to have coffee, anyway.

Call him, some mischievous voice inside her head whispered, daring her to relax, challenging her to at least give him a chance, urging her to step out of the cocoon she had built around her heart or at least make an opening through which some brave soul might find his way in, and Kaylee snorted at the melodrama she'd allowed to go on in her thoughts.

Why was she so nervous about calling him, anyway? It wasn't as if she were calling a guy she was interested in seeing, right? She was only notifying a patron of the shelter that their pet adoption had gone through. So why was her brain making her body feel like she was calling in anticipation of a night in the arms of a devoted lover?

Smoothing her damp palms along her jeans-clad thighs in a misguided attempt to soothe away her sudden attack of nerves, she reached for the phone, flipped to the last page in the folder, found his number, and dialed. He answered on the third ring.

Exhaling slowly, she forced herself to speak calmly although she felt anything but. "Mr. Parker? Hi. It's Kaylee Dean from the animal rescue shelter. I'm calling to let you know the paperwork for your pet adoption went through. You can come by and pick up Sarge whenever you're ready."

Did he hear the slight quiver in her voice? The

way her breath caught and hung on every other word? If so, he didn't let on about it.

"Miss Dean, hello! I was hoping you'd call," he said, and Kaylee shivered with reaction to the warmth which started at her ear and spread outward from the sound. "What time do you close?"

Trying to take her mind off the effect of his voice, Kaylee flipped back through the papers in the folder until her eyes met the space where he had signed his name.

Jordan H. Parker.

Scrawled in black ink in a broad empty box on the white paper, his name stood out in stark relief. It was penned evenly, but somehow still managed to swoop across the page—all flowing and loopy—which was a little unusual for a man's signature. It was intriguing, she thought. Like his eyes. Idly, she wondered what the H stood for, and then realized he was waiting for her reply. She closed the folder. "In about fifteen minutes."

She heard him sigh. "That's not so good. I'm in Center, just outside of town. Not close enough to make it before you lock up. I really wanted to bring Sarge home as soon as possible and I hate to ask, but will tomorrow be okay?"

Disappointment flowed through her. Kaylee hadn't realized how much she'd actually been anticipating seeing him again. She bit back a sigh. "Yes, of course. Tomorrow will be fine."

Only she wouldn't be there tomorrow. Marc would, and … .

Her attention back on the conversation at hand, Kaylee immediately recognized the standard, cordial "thanks for calling" he was giving her now, and that he was getting ready to end the call. Before he could finish and say goodbye, she interrupted him. "Jordan? Um, I mean Mr. Parker?"

"Yes, Miss Dean?" he asked after a slight pause, and she knew she hadn't imagined the slight teasing edge that entered his tone at her having accidentally called him by his first name.

A blush burned her cheeks, but she ignored it. "I'm at the shelter now, but I could meet you at Huntingdon's in half an hour if you'd like. We could do the exchange there."

There was a moment of hesitant silence, then he asked, "Are you sure? It wouldn't be a bother?"

"No bother at all." Certain now that he was going to agree to meet her, she stood and walked to the rack of keys, and selected the one to Sarge's kennel. "I'm sure Sarge is eager to get settled in his new home, and the two of you do seem to have an awful lot to talk about."

Kaylee suddenly wanted to smack herself. The last thing she'd wanted to remind him of was the conversation where he'd asked her out! He'd think she was fishing for another invitation to coffee!

If one could feel a grin of triumph through a simple phone conversation, Kaylee would have sworn she'd felt his when he asked, "Does this mean you'll have coffee with me?"

But she was too busy scolding herself to catch

the note of uncertainty hidden in his question. "It means I'll think about it. See you in half an hour, Mr. Parker."

She ended the call, scooped up the folder, her purse, and pulled on her coat. She'd put everything else in the car first, and then collect Sarge for the ride. It was cold out this evening, and there was no need to make him suffer in it while she got her stuff together.

What a laugh, she thought. If she had her stuff anywhere near together, her hands would not be trembling with uncertainty and her insides would not be quivering, practically giddy with excitement at the thought of seeing Jordan again. Glaring at the dark side of her now closed eyelids, she groaned. Why had she even made the blasted call?

* * *

"Because you want him, chicky," Mortianna said to the vision swirling in front of her before it faded into an inky mist. Turning to Esmerelda, she asked, "Why are these women so scared to admit to their passions?"

"Why are you sneaking down here to eavesdrop on them?" she shot back from the basement doorway. "If Feeny finds out, she's going to kick you out of the coven."

Mortianna stretched and waved away her sister's concern. "She'd have to kick me out of the family first, and we both know she won't do that. She loves me too much. Besides, one of us has to keep an eye on these things. It might as well be me."

"Or you could leave it alone and let their hearts do the work," Serephina offered from behind Esmerelda's shoulder, causing both her sisters to jump guiltily at the sound of her voice.

"Hearts, schmarts. Look what Kaylee's did to her. She let one little episode of broken heartedness shut her down for two years. Two blasted, *wasted* years, Feeny. When are you going to realize that sometimes these romantic entanglements need a little nudging now and again?"

Serephina pushed around Esmerelda and continued down the stairs. "Probably as long as it takes for you to realize a romantic entanglement is not love. *Love* is the prize here, Morty, and it's something that grows out of feelings rooted a lot deeper than a box of chocolates, a dozen roses, and a few hours tussling around on a set of five hundred dollar silk sheets."

"Oooh, is that how much he paid for those?" Morty asked, skirting the issue entirely to dig out the bedding catalog she'd brought down the day after Kaylee and Jordan had made their separate visits to the store while Esmerelda quietly descended the stairs to put away the scrying dish. "I want a set in red, a set in black, and a set in—"

"Your dreams," Serephina finished for her before sweeping the catalog out of her reach. Crossing her arms over her chest, she said, "You're not getting outrageously overpriced silk sheets because you never want to pay for them, and I don't want you spying on Kaylee anymore, okay? If we need to get involved, they will let us know."

Mortianna rolled her eyes. *They* were the modern-day equivalent of a Cupid Heart Guard when clearly what was needed here was the Chief, the big boss, the Love CEO—the top guy himself—not some namby-pamby, seven-man hearts and flowers romance army who thought a couple of magic-infused gifts were an adequate substitute for real passion. Real feeling. Real emotion.

"Fine, fine. I'll stop spying on her. *And* him. I won't peek in on the sexy Mr. Parker, either. I promise." She held out both hands, palm up, in a sign of surrender.

Serephina eyed her suspiciously for a moment, searching for any hint of duplicity. Finding none, she nodded. "Thank you, I think. Now come upstairs and help me with dinner, both of you. I don't want either of you down here without me tonight. You tend to get into trouble when you slip off out of my sight."

"Yes, Mother," Mortianna mocked, and Esmerelda hid a smirk, but both sisters trouped to the stairs, following Serephina up as they were told.

Chapter Five

Jordan was actually nervous, but he'd never admit it—especially not to Sam, who'd been as stunned as he to learn Kaylee had volunteered to meet him at the cafe for coffee.

"Kaylee Dean? You're sure?" Sam asked for the third time since Jordan had mentioned who he was there to meet. He let out a low whistle, then gave Jordan a "way-to-go" shoulder punch. "Never would have thought it'd be you, man."

Jordan turned from his vigil of watching the road for Kaylee's arrival to pin his friend with a questioning stare. "What do you mean?"

"I've seen guys panting after her and a few who probably genuinely cared, but she shot every one of them down without a glance." He held up his finger and thumb like a pistol and kicked it back. "Cold shoulder. Pkew!"

Jordan frowned. "I don't see what that has to do with me. I adopted a dog from the shelter where she works. She agreed to meet me here to do the swap since I was all the way over in Center when she called and wouldn't be able to make it in until tomorrow."

"Uh-huh." Sarcasm practically dripped from his comment. "Bringing the dog, I get. Staying for coffee? Not so much."

He picked up another cup and wiped it dry with a towel, shaking his head in stunned disbelief the entire time. "Has nothing to do with you, man, but that's not Kaylee, dude."

Jordan frowned. Not Kaylee? He didn't even pretend to understand what Sam was talking about. When she'd called from the shelter, she had seemed a little nervous, but weren't all girls nervous when talking to a guy for the first...second...third time? More confused now than he had been a minute ago, he shoved his hands in his pockets and rocked back on his feet. "Sam, if you don't start making sense in about three seconds, I'm about to toss you through this glass, *dude.*"

He said the words casually, nonchalant even, but inside he felt anything but. Was Sam trying to tell him Kaylee Dean had guy issues? If she did, so what? He thought. Practically every woman old enough to take seriously on the planet had some kind of broken heart story to tell. But he sensed that Sam was trying to tell him Kaylee's issues were different. "What's her story?"

Sam shook his head. "I don't know if I should be the one to tell you. Why don't you ask *her* when she gets here?"

Glaring a warning, Jordan said, "Because I'm

asking *you* now. Hey, you started this whole, *"I-can't-believe-Kaylee-Dean-gave-you-the-time-of-day"* thing. It's time to finish it. Why are you so surprised she agreed to meet me?"

"It's her fiance, man. Tore her up real bad." Sam shook his head, put another mug on the shelf and reached for the next one. "It's been four years and she hasn't had a single date that I know of in all that time. I think that Daniel dude really messed with her."

"She's engaged?" Jordan felt cold—from his fingers to his toes—and it had nothing to do with the weather. No wonder she had turned down his invitation to coffee! He let his head fall back against his shoulders, closed his eyes, and huffed out a sigh of disgust. He felt like an idiot now for having asked! "Wait, you knew? Why didn't you *tell* me, Sam?"

Sam was shaking his head. "No, no, she's not engaged. Not now, anyway. But she was. Four years ago. Gonna marry her high-school sweetheart, but he dumped her a month before the wedding. And what do you mean, why didn't I tell you? How was I supposed to know you've been putting the moves on Jo Dean Leavy's little sister?"

The rattle of glass-wear said Sam was a little miffed at his groundless accusation. Jordan lifted his head and started to apologize, but was interrupted.

"Hey, that's her, man," Sam said, motioning toward the parking lot with his towel, and Jordan's eyes snapped back toward the tall glass window, immediately seeking her out. "You gonna go out and meet her or wait for her to come inside?"

Side-eyeing his best buddy since the sixth grade, Jordan shook his head. He liked Sam. For the most part, Sam understood him. He'd been his best friend for half of forever. But just now, he was grating on Jordan's nerves in a bad way.

"Give us five minutes, will you?" he said, and pushed open the door.

Running across the parking lot, he reached to open her door the same time she switched off the engine. "You're early."

"Looks like today's just not my day for getting the timing right." Leaning across to the passenger seat to gather up a heavy black leash and her purse, she turned to look at him, explaining, "This morning, I overslept. Today marks the first time a customer ever had to wait for me to open the shop, and then, I was so busy I missed lunch and was still late getting to the shelter. But what about you? I've just arrived but I could swear you came out of the cafe. Have you been waiting long?"

"Three minutes." Taking the leash from her outstretched hand, he stepped back and waited, holding the door open so she could exit the SUV. "I'll get Sarge. You go on inside. It's freezing out here."

When she hesitated, he arched a brow. "Did I do something wrong?"

After another second's pause during which she bit her lip in hesitation, she shook her head. "He's not used to the cold, since the accident. There's a throw in the back. You'll want to wrap it over him, at least, if you're planning to make him wait in the car."

She turned to reach back inside the vehicle for her coat, and Jordan barely bit back a scoff at her gentle but obvious disapproval of the thought of him leaving Sarge outside, even if he would be inside a vehicle. "I would never leave him to wait in the cold, Miss Dean. Sam said I could bring him into the back room while you and I have coffee—if you haven't changed your mind?"

He cast her a quick, surreptitious glance to measure her reaction to his careful regard for Sarge's needs and to his hopeful assumption that she had definitely agreed to stay for a drink, and noticed her chin was quivering. He grinned.

Ducking back to hide his smile behind the act of closing the car door, he said, "Your teeth are starting to chatter, woman. Get inside where it's warm. Sarge and I will be along in a minute."

It took three, but he'd wrapped the thick, plaid throw from the back of her vehicle over Sarge and carried him inside rather than make the still convalescing dog march across the cold asphalt.

"I'll put him in the back, Sammy," he called out when he stepped inside the cafe with his canine bundle. He joined Kaylee in the dining room a few minutes later. "Got him all settled near the furnace with a bowl of water at his disposal, so he'll be fine. Mind if I sit here?"

Without waiting for her to answer, he pulled out the chair opposite her, and sat, watching while she shrugged off her coat and tried to warm her frozen fingers by putting one hand in the other and then switching them out every few seconds. Pushing his chair back, he stood again. "Coffee will help with that. Do you have a preference, or...?"

"The mocha crème latte is especially good." He grunted in agreement and hurried to the counter to place an order. In less than two minutes, he was back at their table, sliding a cup in her direction before once again taking a seat. "It's steaming, Miss Dean, so watch your fingers."

She thanked him and wrapped both hands immediately around the tall earthenware mug. "I don't know why they're so cold. I usually wear gloves, but I don't think even those would help right now!"

Watching her warm her hands, he leaned back in his seat, quietly sipping at his drink while he studied her more closely, now that they were out of the cold. "You mentioned both a shop and the shelter earlier so I'm guessing you don't actually work full-time at the animal rescue place in town?"

"I volunteer three days a week at the shelter, but my business is pet grooming. I have a little place out on Third Street." She blew across the top of her mug and lifted it to her lips for a quick sip, then asked, "What do *you* do, Mr. Parker? Banking? Real estate?"

"So, I come off as that sort of guy, do I?" Jordan teased, arching a brow in question, but shook his head. "I'm retired. Sold my IT business six months ago and left the *big city* for Hawthorne Grove. Sold my Porsche, bought a house, adopted a dog."

"Really?" Her nose crinkled and her eyes went narrow in a gesture of disbelief. "Forgive me for saying it, but you don't seem like the IT type."

"Not nerdy enough for you?" he asked. "Hold on. I'll run out to the truck and grab my black, horn-rimmed glasses, my super-fast laptop, a handful of micro-ballpoint pens, and a thick plastic pocket protector. Think that'd help?"

"A truck? Now I know you're not into IT, Mr. Parker. Those guys strike me as being much too sportsy-minded to go for the genuine practicality of a truck. The Porsche? That I could believe. But a pick-up?" She paused to sip at her latte, then waved her fingers in his direction. "With that bomber jacket you wear and the dark, flashy sunglasses you had on last week, I'd have thought you were in the spy business."

"Hey, it's not just a *truck*. It's a *Dodge*, and that thing's loaded! It's got a boss V12 engine, and—" It took him a minute to realize she was attempting to tease him back. When he did, Jordan broke off, suddenly feeling as if he'd scored points in a race he hadn't known he'd been running. Leaning forward, he cocked an eyebrow and asked, "Do you find spies attractive, Miss Dean?"

The beginnings of a smile he'd seen flirting at the corners of her lips wilted. "Do you fish for compliments often, Mr. Parker?"

Jordan shifted awkwardly in his chair. Had it been a mistake, he wondered, asking her to join him for coffee? Then, suddenly straightening in his seat, he lifted his head, snapped his fingers, and said, "Wait, I remember now! You're into old stuff, right? Collecting? How could I have forgotten? It's definitely antiques you prefer."

His subtle nudging of her memory back to their first meeting did not go unnoticed. She smiled but shook her head. "Not me. My aunt does. I was shopping for a gift for her last week when you and I ran into each other."

"You mean when *I* ran into *you*. Allow me to apologize—again—for my clumsiness."

"No need," she said, waving away his apology. "I was too busy blabbering into my phone to cousin Mindy about the great find I'd picked up to notice we were on a collision course myself. If you hadn't bumped into me when you did, I'm sure it would have been *me* who bowled *you* over."

She looked directly at him then, and he felt something tighten, low and heavy, in his gut. "I think maybe you have anyway, Miss Kaylee Dean."

The change in his voice would have been hard for anyone to miss. Kaylee heard it, and he knew she even recognized it for what it was: he was attracted to her. Worse for her though, he suspected, was that she felt drawn to him also. Glancing down at her hands where they wrapped tightly around her mug, she said, "Jordan, I appreciate the coffee and I didn't mind bringing Sarge out at all, but—"

"Don't."

Recognizing the direction her sudden speech was heading, Jordan reached across the table and covered her hands, holding them in place around the mug beneath his. He paused, waiting until she looked up at him again to release them, and then said, "It's just coffee, Kaylee. Nothing serious, nothing to be afraid of, and definitely nothing to run away from."

"See?" Holding his hands in the air, he twisted them back and forth. "No strings."

After a moment, she offered a hesitant nod and relaxed back in her chair. "Alright. Just coffee. I think I can do that."

Not daring to let her see how relieved he felt at her acceptance of him in her life, for the moment at least, Jordan smiled. "Now that we have that out of the way, how do you feel about movies?"

Tilting her head slightly, she paused with her latte half-way to her mouth. "Are you asking me to see a movie with you, or my thoughts on them, in general?"

Feeling a little sheepish for pushing forward so quickly after having assured her she had no reason to worry that he was trying to make a move on her, he shrugged and admitted, "To see one with me."

Her brow rose, and he held up his hands, halting her refusal before she could give it. "But it's not what you think."

"Oh?" He heard her quiet little snort, but there was still a mixture of surprise, disbelief, curious interest, and even a bit of humor in her expression when she finished with, "Please, feel free to take a moment to explicate how it is not."

"I don't know anybody." Leaning forward, he

entreated, "I'm new here, remember? I don't know any of the people—well, except for Sam, but he always wants to talk through the best scenes. Then, there are the whispers showing up at the movies with him would start that I just don't want to deal with. Forgive me for being sensitive about it, but no way am I asking him."

Kaylee swirled her drink in the mug. "You left out the part about how this is not you asking me out for a movie date."

She had him there. He crossed his arms over his chest and leaned back, hoping she couldn't see through the calm facade he hoped he was projecting to the man who was still allergic to rejection underneath. "That's because I *am*, but if you'll say yes, I promise not to expect you to drive me home after, or to kiss me goodnight at the door before you leave. Fair enough?"

Her laughter floated into the almost awkward silence, surprising them both. Her cheeks flushed with color and she lowered her gaze. "I think I might actually enjoy a night at the movies, Mr. Parker, but—"

Quickly, before she could finish, he held up his hands again, reminding her there would be no strings, and she smiled. "No strings. Right."

"I promise," he said. "Just a guy and a girl enjoying a silly old chick flick and some popcorn together."

"You want to watch a silly old chick flick?" She asked, side-eyeing him with a hint of rebellion in her gaze.

"Not my fault, or even my preference. Just happens to be the only things playing at the theater right now, okay? How's Saturday night? We can meet here at seven." When she hesitated, he arched a brow. "Come on, Kaylee Dean. It's just a movie. What do you say? Will you help a new guy out?"

"Yes," she said after a pause so long Jordan thought he might actually start to perspire in preparation for rejection anxiety. "Yes, I think I will."

Chapter Six

By the time Thursday afternoon rolled around, Kaylee was ready to call the whole thing off.

Hefting the linens bag off her shoulder and into the back of her car, she closed the door with a little more force than necessary and marched to open the front one. Exasperated, she tossed her purse into the passenger seat and slid behind the wheel. A few minutes later, she maneuvered into traffic, headed for the cleaners to drop off today's towels and things and pick up fresh ones for tomorrow, her thoughts still spinning.

She should have called and canceled the movie date with Jordan Parker as soon as she'd gotten home on Monday. If one more member of her family—extended or otherwise—congratulated her for finally putting her past in the past and moving on from what had been one of the most emotionally tragic moments of her life, she would.

For a minute, she imagined she could see his expression when she called him to say she had changed her mind and even the imaginary flash of pain she pretended she could see in those sexy eyes of his made her wince. Darn it, why couldn't everyone just leave her alone about it?

Why couldn't they understand she was telling the truth when she told them she and Jordan were only going to be at the movies together because he was new here and wanted to familiarize himself with the local surroundings? He'd only recently moved to Hawthorne Grove. Like he'd said, it wasn't as if he could pick up the phone and call any one of a score of people nearby like she could and ask them to join him. There was only Sam Huntingdon, and she couldn't blame him for preferring his first visit to The Grove Cinema be with a female—especially given that this Saturday was couples night—which was why they were only playing romantic comedies. But the more her family and circle of friends who called congratulated her on her decision to go out, the more Kaylee thought doing so might be another of those Very Bad Ideas she occasionally had.

It took less than five minutes to do the drop off and pick up at Dee's Linen and More. In six, she was back on the road, a quarter hour from home, and her thoughts—as they had been all week—were on her upcoming date with Jordan again.

Obviously, her friends were reading more into the casual night out than they should, and she had almost expected that. Her family, however—she'd really thought they understood why she'd removed herself from the singles scene for the past four years and why she had no plans for ever going back in.

Daniel.

The heart-breaker.

The dream-killer.

The sweetest, most tender, wonderful love of her life who had broken off their engagement the day she'd hurried to his apartment from work to show him her wedding dress. For six months, she'd saved to buy that specific dress. Her entire goal? To be the most beautiful bride possible for the world's most perfect man.

She'd believed he deserved it.

They'd been together all through high-school. They were so obviously meant for each other, they'd been voted Couple Most Likely in their senior year. For four years, he was there for her, and she had truly believed they would be together forever. He'd even been waiting for her at the door when she ran up the steps to his apartment, a smile on her lips, sparkles in her eyes, and her heart spilling over from the sheer happiness she'd felt in that moment.

Looking back, she could only guess her own emotions had blinded her completely to seeing the lack of his, which was why she had made a promise to herself to never get so emotionally involved she could not see what was right in front of her face ever again.

At home, she unlocked the door to her small, one-bedroom apartment and then nudged it shut with her heel without bothering to lock it again. Hawthorne Grove's crime rate was practically nonexistent. Everyone knew everyone here—well, except for Jordan Parker, and now she was obligated by her own words to try and help him change that.

After putting her purse and keys aside and slipping out of her coat, Kaylee went to rummage through the fridge and cabinets in the kitchen. She might be exasperated with the way her family was treating this thing with Jordan, but she still had to eat. She decided on a salad. With any luck, she'd be able to finish it before Jo called.

Her sister was the only one who hadn't yet phoned or dropped by to quiz her about the mystery man she was going out with Saturday who had, reportedly, swept her off her feet. Kaylee snorted at her family's misguided romantic fantasies. Jordan was more like to knock her over than sweep her up, if their first meeting was any to go by.

Without effort, her mind drew an image of him the way she'd first seen him, complete with bomber jacket and dark glasses, and she smiled. He *was* a cutey, if she were honest about it. In fact, he was downright hot. If cousin Mindy ever crossed his path, she'd be flat out drooling. But then, she reminded herself, Min had found Daniel drool-worthy, too.

While she put together several leafy greens, some onion, shredded cheese, ham squares, and a handful of croutons in a bowl, her thoughts drifted back to the last time she'd spoken to Daniel Smith.

Wedding dress day.

She had hurried to meet him at the door, pressing an exuberant kiss to his cheek without noticing his less than enthusiastic response as she pushed inside his apartment. But she had noticed everything he said and did shortly thereafter. It was as if the entire world had slowed to a crawl and no matter how desperately she had wanted to in that moment, time itself would not allow her to run and hide.

"I've met someone" was his answer when she'd giddily asked if he wanted to see the gown she'd be wearing when she became the luckiest woman in the world. "I never expected it to happen this way, but I hope someday you will understand" were the last words he'd spoken before leaving her alone, utterly dumb-founded and confused, to meet his girlfriend at the airport in Center.

That day was one of the most exciting and thoroughly devastating days of her life. It still affected her badly, even two years later, when she thought about it. Cruel as memories often are, hers from the day of the breakup were downright ruthless, and all this happy chatter from her family and friends over her innocent acceptance of an invitation to see a movie with Jordan Parker was bringing back every one she'd ever had, in vivid, bleeding color.

What little she'd had of an appetite vanished. A sigh of disappointment slid past her lips and she got up to toss the uneaten half of her salad into the disposal. Frowning now, she flipped the switch, then rinsed her plate and fork before setting them aside to wash later, suddenly wishing she could get rid of her memories of Daniel as easily as she had her dinner.

Still lost in thought, she left the kitchen, wandering semi-dazed through the living room until she was standing behind the sofa, looking down at the table where she'd put the beautiful water globe from Seville's. Gently, she lifted it from the stand. Despite the frozen scene depicted inside, the glass was warm in her hands. Her mind was still plagued but the heat from the ball was soothing. Carrying it with her, she rounded the sofa and sat, legs tucked beneath her, and quietly contemplated the cozy imagery inside.

Why did everyone seem to think she'd forgotten? The humiliation, the agony, the thousands upon thousands of tears? The endless days she'd spent curled in a lonely, miserable ball in the middle of her bed because she was too heart-stricken to go out, to be seen in public? It had taken her weeks to recover enough from the shame to show up as a volunteer at the shelter again, and months passed before she'd felt confident enough to reopen her grooming shop in town, but nothing felt the same.

Daniel's desertion just weeks before their wedding day had almost ruined her. Everyone who knew her and knew how badly the breakup had affected her also knew she had no plans to ever put herself in a position to feel such an unspeakable depth of anguish, ever again. But she'd said yes when the new guy in town asked her to sit with him through a movie and her family acted like she'd announced another engagement!

Staring, mostly unseeing, down at the snow globe through eyes glazed with a sheen of unshed tears, Kaylee tilted the glass ball from side to side then turned it over to stir up the white flakes inside and watched, dazed, for the hundredth time since she'd gotten home this evening as it trickled slowly down.

How could they? How could they expect her to even pretend she was ready to attempt the whole relationship thing again? Romantic entanglements were the last thing she was interested in and her family and friends should know that. This thing with Jordan was only about being a good citizen, a friendly neighbor, so to speak. She was helping him to adjust, to acclimate to a new town, new places, and new people. Plus, he'd promised no strings. If she thought, even for a minute, that he had expectations for the evening, she would call and cancel immediately, but ...

Oh, for grief's sake, Kaylee! Why don't you stop pretending? Stop analyzing and just admit it! It's not your family being happy you're going out again that bothers you. The truth is, you're afraid. You know Jordan Parker asked you out because he obviously feels that ... that something that wants to sizzle between the two of you when you're together, and you are terrified of having said yes to him because you feel it, too!

* * *

On the outskirts of town, in a smallish two-story ranch nestled cozily in the center of a small grove of aged hawthorn trees, Jordan stared down with a feeling of utter dissatisfaction at the newly restored and finally dry antique letter box sitting open on the newspaper lined work table in front of him.

After days of carefully dismantling, sanding, tediously replacing broken bits and pieces before rejoining and refinishing the whole, he knew the antique box likely rivaled its original beauty, but just as with the score of other pieces he had collected and restored over the past ten years, there was no real sense of accomplishment, no fulfilling sense of completion now that the work was done.

With a sigh, he picked up the finished box and headed in from the garage to put it in the place he'd cleared for it yesterday on the mantel in his living room. Maybe Stacy was right. Maybe it was time he stopped wasting time on trying to put broken things from the past back together as good as or better than they were before and started working on the future—his future.

Whistling for Sarge, he closed the garage door and went through the back door to the living room —the only room in the house with a fully functioning fireplace. Carefully sliding the box onto the mantel, he raised the lid, then closed it again. There was nothing inside it, the same as there was nothing to put into the eighteen other similar boxes he had spread around the house. So why did he continue to buy them? What, exactly, was it that drew him to the darn things in the first place?

According to his ex-girlfriend, he was obsessed. The fact that the boxes he collected were actually valuable antiques had held no significance to her. Aside from restoration, he did nothing with them. Other than supposedly gaining value as long as time continued to pass, the boxes served no purpose and had no discernible function other than to sit—useless and empty—wherever he placed them.

Dust collectors, that's what Stacy had called them. How often had he heard her complain about their presence in his apartment, claiming the only things they were good for was to collect dust and take up valuable table space—space he theoretically could have used for other, more serviceable purposes—like to display half a dozen half-empty bottles of nail polish, or several glossy brochures of expensive, exotic places to which he had no intention of traveling but where Stacy plotted and schemed to get him to go, or to store piles of colorful unfolded feminine underwear.

Drumming his thumb in agitation against the mantel, Jordan seriously considered packing the boxes up again, including the new one. It had been almost two weeks since he'd made the purchase and he still wasn't sure why he had done so. But when he glanced again at the box on the mantel, every inch of the exterior wooden surface newly polished and glowing with a rich, warm, amber-gold sheen, he immediately decided against it.

Right now, he had more important things to do —like drive over to Sammy's for coffee. Sam had an old *chiffonier* he'd gotten at an estate sale a year or so ago that was missing a couple doors and some of the drawers were falling apart. He wanted Jordan to have a look at it and he'd promised free coffee as payment.

Sam probably wanted to pester him some more about getting into the antique restoration business, too, but Jordan had no intention of listening. He hadn't been teasing Kaylee when he'd told her about selling the IT business. He had enjoyed it, but it had taken a lot out of him, too. He wasn't sure he was ready to jump back into the business world again. Besides, putting a few old boxes back together was one thing, but reconstructing vintage furniture was another thing entirely.

Grabbing his coat, he whistled for Sarge again and headed out, locking the door behind him. At the truck, he opened the door and bent to help Sarge into the cab. "Come on, boy. Sammy's waiting."

During the drive, he kept thinking about the boxes, about his reasons for collecting them, about why he couldn't seem to find a real use for them, but at the same time, he didn't want to let them go. Answers continued to elude him, but he did manage to come up with a viable solution. If he didn't find a use for the letter boxes soon, he promised himself, he would get rid of them—*all* of them—even if the only way he could make himself do it was to gift them to his family and friends as birthday presents.

Chapter Seven

Seven o'clock Saturday evening was only three minutes away by the time Kaylee pulled into the parking lot at Huntingdon's and shut off her engine. Deep in her gut, she had a feeling tonight's outing (it was not a date, after all) with Jordan wasn't going to go well, but she hadn't called to cancel, so standing him up at the last minute was out of the question.

Gathering her purse and jacket, she noticed several familiar vehicles: Jo and Michael were both here, and so was Mindy and Lain and even Marc. Add one from Jordan's side of the "friend or family" to include Sam and Kaylee felt like a freak specimen on display. With an effort of will, she pushed aside her irritation and the disquieting agitation she felt and started inside.

She was half-way to the door when Jordan walked out.

"It's kind of crowded in there," he said after they exchanged greetings. "But given the time, I suppose you weren't interested in grabbing a coffee anyway. Were you?"

"No." She didn't elaborate and he didn't seem to need her to. Nodding, he motioned toward a vehicle parked near the edge of the lot under a big oak tree. "We can head out whenever you're ready."

Shouldering her purse, Kaylee started in the direction he had indicated. "I'm ready now."

Five minutes later, they were standing in line for drinks and popcorn at The Grove Cinema. In ten, they were seated and waiting for the movie to start, but Kaylee wasn't paying much attention to the screen. Instead, she was biting back the few choice words she wanted to shout every time she saw one of her acquaintances move down the center aisle, grinning and waving in her direction. They had followed her, the cretins.

"Hey, why the scowl?" Jordan asked. "The show's just getting started."

He popped a handful of popcorn in his mouth and settled back in his seat, getting comfortable for the viewing, but Kaylee couldn't make herself relax enough to do more than sit, ramrod straight and fuming, in her chair. Were they planning to watch her all night? An irritated sigh slipped out.

"This is ridiculous," she muttered under her breath. To Jordan, she said, "Sorry. I just remembered something I forgot to do at home."

He stopped chewing and sat up. "Is it important? I can drive you over if you left the stove on or something."

"No, it's nothing that can't wait," she said,

waving him back. Tomorrow, however, a few people were going to get phone calls they'd probably rather skip.

"Great. Here, have some popcorn." There was a note of mischief in his tone and when she turned to accept the cup of warm, buttery popped kernels from him, she found out why. He tossed a particularly fluffy piece at her lips. It bounced off, of course, and landed in her lap, where he eyed it carefully before looking up at her face again. "Ah, I'd risk retrieving that and try again if I didn't think you'd smack me half-way into next week, but..."

One corner of his lips rose in a wry smile. Kaylee blinked, then blinked again. Why had he thrown popcorn at her?

"You're tense, Miss Dean, and tonight isn't supposed to make you jumpy," he explained. "Was it something I said?"

There was both curiosity and mischief in his gaze and for the life of her, Kaylee wasn't sure how to respond to either. It wasn't his fault her friends were nosy. Nor had he asked them to follow her. She shook her head. "It's just that I don't go out often anymore."

Crunching another handful of popcorn, Jordan nodded. "I know how you feel. It's been six months —no, make that eight—since I last stepped inside a movie theater but who can resist the popcorn, right? There's nothing like movie theater popcorn. Mmm!"

Again, that teasing gleam in his eye tempted her

to respond in kind. Relaxing a bit in response to his playful attitude, Kaylee managed a smile and reached for a handful before retrieving the errant piece from her lap. "I haven't been here in almost three years. Nothing's changed, though, that I can see."

Turning her head, she looked around to verify her words, and her gaze clashed head-on with her sister's, one row back and three seats to her right. Beside her, Michael tipped his head and grinned. She groaned, then mouthed, "Jo? What are you doing here?"

A mistake, she realized immediately, because Jo stood, leaving her seat to move closer to Kaylee. Once she found a suitable spot behind her sister, Jo leaned up and met Kaylee's squint-eyed glare with one of her own.

"Don't you dare lump me in with *them*," she whispered loudly, motioning to the other side of the theater where the others sat. "I didn't come here to spy. It's date night for Michael and I and we always do the cinema during Couples Night."

Kaylee immediately felt sorry for having done precisely as Jo had accused. She glanced around and found Jordan sitting with his head twisted to the side, avidly following their conversation. Against her better judgment, she decided she might as well introduce them.

"Jordan Parker, this is my sister, Jo Leavy. Jo, Jordan Parker." Waving toward her brother-in-law, she leaned close and whispered, "And that's her husband, Michael."

Jordan nodded, smiled, and reached back with buttery fingers to shake hands, then snatched his hand back to reach over with the other.

"Popcorn," he explained sheepishly, keeping his voice low so as not to disturb the other viewers. "It's a pleasure to meet you, Mrs. Leavy. Michael."

Jo smiled. "You, too, Mr. Parker. And now that I've saved myself an ear-blistering phone call tomorrow, I'm going to go back to making out with my date!"

Kaylee's eyes widened and she could feel her cheeks flush, but Jordan, who was staring even more curiously at her now, only grinned. "Wow. Your sister and brother-in-law still make out at movies? They must seriously be in love!"

"She's only teasing," Kaylee whispered after her sister had gone, but she couldn't resist a quick glance over her shoulder to make sure.

Jordan sputtered with barely subdued laughter. "Ignore them, Kaylee. Older siblings live to embarrass younger ones but we don't have to give them the pleasure."

Sinking slightly in her seat, Kaylee nodded. He'd guessed right—she was embarrassed, but not by Jo, or Michael, or even Marc and his date, and Mindy and hers, who were barely three rows back to their right. Instead, she was very much chagrined to realize the reason she had been so upset to see her friends and family both here and at Huntingdon's was because she wasn't prepared to bear their scrutiny. She hadn't been out in more than four years—perhaps she had forgotten how one was supposed to behave?

Looking around at the other couples, she saw them dipping into shared cups of popcorn and leaning close now and again to whisper low—quiet threads of conversation kept low just like hers and Jordan's had been a moment ago. Satisfied she hadn't made any blunders, she turned her attention to the screen, but the movie was barely more than halfway through when she realized without a doubt that tonight had been a mistake.

It had nothing to do with Jordan or her friends and family but everything to do with the romance playing out on the screen. The male lead was scared. He was leaving. The female lead was upset, but Kaylee was worse. In the movie, she knew the guy was going to come back, but in real life—in real life it didn't happen.

When the movie ended, she barely said a thing as she gathered her things. Somehow, she managed not to spill her drink or topple her cup of popcorn in her rush to get to her feet. Beside her, Jordan stood up and stretched, content to loiter while the credits rolled, looking for all the world as if he were in no hurry to leave.

"Come on," she whispered, and grabbed at his hand before making her way up the side aisle. Behind her, she could hear her not-date date for the evening hurrying to catch up, but she didn't wait. In the lobby, she quickly slid into her coat and headed up the sidewalk toward the park, ignoring the fact that Jordan's truck was parked behind her in the other direction.

"Kaylee, hold up." Jordan called, but she only shook her head. She couldn't stop. Not yet. She was too irritated, too emotional. He would expect her to explain, and given that she'd rushed him out of the cinema, she would owe him that much, at least. But not now. Her emotions were wired, and the words probably wouldn't come.

She was wrong.

"Kaylee?"

He'd caught up to her and reached out to halt her flight. His hand landed somewhere in the vicinity of her neck instead of the shoulder he'd obviously meant to catch, and his touch—the warmth of his strong, bare fingers, the way he'd compensated for missing her shoulder by curling his hand to splay his fingers into her hair, and the gentle way he used his thumb to caress the line of her jaw as she turned—sent her barreling headlong down a path she'd never meant to tread.

Looking up at him, eyes wide, she asked, "How can the directors live with themselves? It's all *lies.* All of it. Real life never works that way, and you *know* they have to know it. They do! So why do they pretend? Why encourage us to make believe along with them through stupid, gushy movies like that one? Why?"

Jordan couldn't know she was talking about the brokenhearted lovers on the screen, couldn't guess she'd become upset because the hero of the piece had walked out on his heroine, the same as Daniel had done to her, only there had been no happy ending for the two of them like there was for the leads in the movie.

He remained silent, but then, given how confused he must be about what had set her off to begin with, what *could* he say? So he said nothing, and did the next best thing instead. Without removing his fingers from her nape, he reached out with his other hand to pull her against his chest, into his embrace, and simply held her close for a moment.

Kaylee welcomed his warmth, the comfort and sense of security she felt while he held her in his arms so much she didn't even think about what she was doing or with whom. She simply held on for dear life, her fingers clenched in the material of his dark shirt beneath his open coat, while she quietly relived all the pain and anguish of her own real-life heartbreak with her head on his shoulder as she stared off into the night.

"He came back before the end of the movie. The hero. Right when she thought he never would, and everything was alright for them. He told her he was wrong, that he loved her, and she had to confess that she still loved him, too. Their world was complete."

Her snort of disdain was muffled by his shirt, but she continued. "In ninety minutes, all was set to rights and you know there was a happily ever after for them." Pushing slightly back out of his embrace, she gazed up at him and said, "But it never happens that way for us. Not in real life, for real people. Never."

For a long moment, he simply stared at her, his

fingers doing things in her hair while he studied her face in silence.

"It does, Kaylee," he finally said, and she blinked, surprised more by the confidence in his tone than his actual words.

"When?" she demanded. "When does it happen, Jordan Parker?"

Looking away, she shook her head in denial. "Forgive me for disbelieving you, but I'm afraid you'll have to prove it, because right now I don't think I'll ever believe anyone about it ever again."

"When it's real," he stated simply, quietly, and something in his voice made her look at him again. Everything inside her went still. There was something in his eyes, in the way he was looking at her when he spoke that made her breath catch.

Reaching out, he smoothed an errant strand of her hair back from her cheek and tucked it gently behind her ear. "They come back when love is real, Kaylee, I promise. Every. Single. Time."

There was such sincerity in his tone, so much certainty in his gaze, she found his words hard to refute. It was obvious he truly believed what he had said, and so, for the moment, she found herself believing it, too.

Kaylee couldn't say precisely what happened to her in her thoughts, in her heart and head in that moment to make her reach up to him, or what made her curl her fingers around his neck, threading them through his hair much the way his had done in hers just moments before.

She couldn't explain why she rose up on her

toes, allowing her body to mold itself to his right there beneath the streetlights half-way between the Grove Cinema and Hawthorne Park.

She didn't even pretend to understand the mixed courses of emotion and reaction flowing through her right then. But one thing she did know, without a doubt—the moment her lips touched his, she was lost.

Chapter Eight

Jordan had known from the minute he'd first seen Kaylee tonight that something was bothering her. She'd seemed agitated on the drive over from Sam's and her tension had only gotten worse as they'd waited for the movie to start.

From what her sister had said, he gathered her annoyance had something to do with her friends but he didn't think they were responsible for what was happening now. He had a feeling this was tied to her ex-fiance somehow and the movie they'd been watching had brought her emotions rushing to the fore. Still, he couldn't deny he was enjoying the moment.

Slowly, he let his arms come around her, his hands supporting, consoling, without actually holding her. He was afraid if he tried to gather her into his embrace the way his body was urging him to do, she would bolt in sheer panic, so he held her lightly and gave her the lead, which she took.

Her fingers threaded through the hair at his nape while her lips closed over his. The kiss was not a hungry one, fueled by passion or anger or pain. Instead, it was more of an exploration.

Soft, slow, she brushed her parted lips against his.

Questing.

Feeling.

Absorbing.

Her tentative, gentle seeking was causing reactions he hadn't expected and when he felt her tongue slide over the fullness of his bottom lip, he almost forgot he was letting her control the moment. His instinctive urge was to pull her close, to plunge into her mouth, to suckle and devour her sweetness. Instead, he forced his hands to remain where they were and responded in kind.

He heard her swift intake of breath an instant before her mouth opened more fully over his, inviting his tongue inside. His long-denied passions having been ignited, Jordan was more than willing to oblige. Bringing his hands up to cup her jaw, he deepened the kiss, plundering the softness of her mouth with his own. His fingers slid upward, tangling in her hair while he tasted her, their tongues sliding together in a rhythm-less dance that transported them both into a world of their own making.

Time slipped away.

How long they stood there, bodies close and lips fused, he did not know. The only thing he was conscious of at that moment was how good she felt in his arms, how sweet she tasted, and how right it felt to be with her there.

Breaking away slightly so he could taste more of her, Jordan placed a trail of little kisses from the corner of her lips up to her earlobe where he nibbled for a moment before sliding further down to taste the curve of shadowed skin where her neck and shoulder met.

She shivered from the contact and he lifted his head to see her reaction. The molten passion he saw in her eyes, in her expression, jolted him back to awareness and he reminded himself of the promise he had made to her for the evening: no strings.

He had to stop.

Swallowing back his groan of disappointment, he reached up, cupping her jaw in his palm. He would ask. He had promised her no strings and even though she had been the one to instigate the kiss, he would let her choose whether or not to go on, to further explore this searing new passion that had unexpectedly flared high and bright between them.

"Kaylee?"

Her eyes started to focus, the passion he saw in her gaze began to wane, and he speared his fingers through her hair, holding her for another quick kiss. But his conscience would not allow him to continue and he broke away with a sigh.

"Kaylee, I would love nothing more than to hold you and kiss you for hours, but—and please don't take this the wrong way—I need you to want it, too." He leaned in for another sip. "Is it okay for me to kiss you?"

Again, he let his lips move softly against hers, allowed his tongue to rim the edges closest to the warm sweetness of her mouth before he leaned back again, putting the barest space between them. "I know I promised no strings tonight and I meant it, but—you're all fire in my arms and I suddenly rather desperately want to do things with your mouth, but you have to tell me it's okay. Kaylee? Baby, you're killing me here."

He sensed her withdrawal before he felt it in the slight stiffening of her arms before she pulled her hands away and took a step back to stare up at him, hesitant and momentarily dazed. The look of bewildered confusion in her gaze swiftly gave way to one of horror and abject humiliation. Drawing her arms around herself, she backed away, putting even more space between them.

"Oh my God, I'm sorry. I—I don't know what came over me, but I—I am so sorry, Jordan."

"Don't," he said, reaching out to stay her words more than her flight. "I'm not sorry and neither should you be."

His fingers curled around her shoulders, pulling her to him until his forehead rested against hers. He couldn't resist planting a quick kiss on the end of her pert, slightly upturned little nose. "You taste like a dream, Kaylee Dean. A promise that is all sweetness and fire. Innocence, and passion, and pure bliss, and I—I loved every minute of it, so don't you dare apologize."

Her expression turned rueful and she cut her eyes away, avoiding his gaze. "So much for no strings, huh?"

Jordan smiled. "Hey, is that what your fingers were doing back there in my hair?"

The sound she uttered was some kind of cross between a snort and a laugh, and her cheeks were still flushed—whether from their kisses or embarrassment, he didn't know—but he was glad she hadn't run away or demanded he take her home immediately.

Sliding his hands into his pockets, he stepped back a couple steps. "Are you cold?" he asked solicitously. "If you are, we should head back. But if you're not, we could walk. I don't think I've seen the park yet. You could show me around."

"There's not much to see in the dark."

"So we'll talk," he suggested. Surprisingly, she didn't refuse. She started forward and he fell into step beside her, content for the moment just to be with someone instead of having to spend what was left of the evening at home alone.

"I guess you're wondering what's wrong with me, right?"

He glanced sideways at her. "What do you mean?"

She rolled her eyes. "Well, first, I blow off your requests to take me to coffee and give you the cold shoulder, then I pretty much force you to reconsider your offer to buy me a mocha latte, and I follow that up by making a fool of myself over a movie and acting like a wounded little girl before mauling you with kisses in the dark."

Jordan grinned and nudged her shoulder with

his. "Hey, you can maul me with kisses any time you feel up to it. I won't complain, I swear!"

She fell silent for long moments, then glanced up at him. "I was engaged."

Jordan's gaze flickered to hers and he paused for a moment to say, "Considering what we just shared, let me be the first to express my gratitude that you said enga*ged*, as in past tense."

He was careful to keep his tone light. He didn't want to admit Sam had already told him about her past, so he held his silence, and moved on. If she wanted to tell him more, she would.

"Four years ago, Daniel and I were a month from —" She dragged in a breath and then continued. "From making what would have been the biggest mistake of our lives. I didn't know that at the time, but he—he'd met someone else. He fell in love with someone else, and he left—three weeks before our wedding."

Jordan stopped, his eyes searching hers, though he hadn't a clue what he was looking for. Pain, he supposed, but that was obvious. Maybe he was hoping to see indifference? "That must have been very difficult for you."

"Very." She started walking again. "In fact, things were so bad I kind of shut myself away. Trying to hide from the hurt, you know? But it didn't work."

"How long were the two of you together?"

"Since high school. We were like the couples you read about in fairy tales. Everyone expected us to get married and we were so close. I'd already bought my wedding gown."

"It didn't happen, obviously, but like everyone else, I expected it to. When Daniel broke our engagement and for a long time after, I was lost. I'd always expected to become Daniel's wife, and when he left, I didn't know what to do."

"You look like you've recovered nicely. A business in town. Volunteering at the shelter. Shopping for cousins who like to drop in on you unexpectedly at the movies to catch a glimpse of your smokin' hot date." She glanced over at him and he grinned until her brow rose questioningly. He shrugged. "Your sister mentioned not having come to the cinema to spy on you, so I gathered that was what you believed your cousin had done."

"Mmm, yes. Mindy. And Marc, another volunteer who works part-time at the shelter."

"You were angry with them?"

"I was, yes," she nodded. "But it seems kind of silly now, considering the rest."

"Ah, yes, your kiss mauling," he teased, and she nudged him with her shoulder.

Giving him a mock glare, she said, "Will you stop? I'm trying to explain, to prove I'm not completely insane in case there's a chance you'd like to try this whole night at the movies thing again."

"I don't think you're insane, Kaylee. I think you were hurt in the past, annoyed with your friends for being so insensitive to what you are trying to do in the present, and then the movie brought back memories of things you'd rather not deal with right now." He shrugged. "I figure it was just too much for you to handle at the moment."

"What do *you* think I am trying to do?" she asked, latching on to that bit of what he had said.

Jordan shrugged. "Start over? Take back your life? To figure out it's okay to live and love again despite the pain you felt over losing Daniel."

She stared inquisitively at him for a long time, speculating. Trying to dissect him, he thought. Figure out what made him tick. Finally, she must have arrived at a conclusion because she said, "You're pretty clever, Jordan Parker."

"Thank you. You're fairly clever yourself, Kaylee Dean."

She laughed and then hugged herself, rubbing against her arms to try and warm them. "It's freezing out here!"

Holding his coat open in invitation for her to cuddle at his side if she wanted to, Jordan sighed. "If only I hadn't left Sarge with Sammy. I could have whistled for him to bring the truck around, but now we'll have to walk."

Kaylee stepped close and giggled at his silliness. "How is he, by the way?"

"Sammy?" he asked, as if he didn't know she'd been asking about the dog.

She rolled her eyes. "No, Sarge. Is he getting around easier lately or are his injuries still slowing him down."

Jordan moved closer to her to share whatever heat was available, smiling into the night in relief at how easily she had moved past her embarrassment over having kissed him earlier. "Well, if you'll agree to meet us here tomorrow when it's daylight, you can see for yourself."

She went quiet, and he glanced down. Their eyes met and held.

"You really want to see me again?"

He nodded.

"Definitely. Again, and again, and again. Sarge wants to see you, too. Told me so himself before I let him out at Sam's. Will you say yes?" There was a twinkle of merriment in her eyes and he felt an odd sort of thrill to know she was happy in the moment because of him.

"How could I say no to Sarge?"

* * *

"Whew! Yowzaa, that was some kiss," Mortianna said, fanning herself with her hand. "If only good old Jordie's conscience hadn't got the better of him, we might have needed ice water after that one."

"Mmm. Or a cold shower, at least." Serephina agreed as she walked over to the couch and sat down with her legs tucked under her. Carefully, she lifted a cup of hot tea to her lips. "But now you see, right? They don't need nudging. If we leave them alone, everything will work out fine."

"Do you really have to turn every viewing into a lecture, Feeny?" Mortianna asked while scowling down at her wet nails. She'd only managed to polish three when Kaylee got on her toes to kiss

Jordan and somehow, she'd managed to smudge one.

"Well, no, actually. After these many years I shouldn't think I'd need to but you insist on trying to meddle and you've even brought Merry in on your little schemes. You think I can't see when you flick your wrists or blink or wave your dainty little fingers here and there?"

With a wistful sigh, Esmerelda moved to put away the scrying dish, ignoring the crooked, devious little smile curving Mortianna's lips as she drew the nail brush down the length of a nail. She had done something. Esmerelda was sure of it. But there was no way in all Witchdom she was about to let on about what she knew.

Besides, Feeny usually managed to make her fess up, and she had little doubt tonight would be different from any other viewing wherein Morty decided to break the rules.

Personally, Esmerelda didn't care how they managed to get the humans together, so long as they did it. After twenty seven long and grueling years of couple-pairing, she could only hope they were nearing the end of their term. Or getting close to making their quota. Or coming to whatever conclusion it was that they needed to meet before this whole Enchanted Hearts for All deal was done for good.

It was all part of *the Cupid Pact*, she knew, but neither she nor her sisters were getting any younger and she, for one, was ready to have a try at enjoying a life of her own. A love of her own. A chance to know how it felt to be fulfilled and happy and cared for by someone who was not in her immediate family.

Pushing the dish into place, she closed the cabinet doors and flipped the warded catch closed by rote, still deeply lost in thought. Just how long *had* it been since she, or Morty, or even Serephina had had their own little slice of romance to nibble on?

Chapter Nine

At a quarter past noon, Kaylee glanced up from the book she had been reading while finishing off her lunch. She'd heard a loud bark in the distance and raised her head, staring out over the park toward the parking area beyond the trees.

It had to be Sarge; the bark sounded so familiar. But she still couldn't see either him or Jordan for the trees and the fence blocking her view of the lot. This late into winter, most of the trees were bare but the evergreens and the trunks of the old oaks lining the park were large and effectively obscured her view.

The sound came again and this time she knew it was Jordan bringing Sarge, whether she could see them or not. Sticking a bookmark into the paperback she'd been reading, she laid it on the bench beside her, stood up to pat her hands against her thighs and call out. "Sarge! Come on, Sarge!"

"Oh, wow. You're doing much better now, aren't you, boy?" she asked a moment later, briskly ruffling her fingers through the cream and sand colored fur on his sides when he ran into view and finally jumped up to give her a big, happy doggie kiss in greeting.

"I think it's the Woofy treats Sam keeps slipping him when I'm not looking," Jordan explained, sauntering up more slowly than Sarge had. He thumbed the retractable leash into a locked position so Sarge could go no further than a few feet away and gestured toward the book and the fast food bag on the bench where she'd been sitting. "Have you been waiting long?"

Kaylee shook her head and reached over to slide her book and the remains of her lunch aside. "About fifteen minutes, but I used the time to get caught up on some reading, so it's all good."

Jordan glanced at the cover of what was clearly a romance novel and his lips twisted wryly. "Real quality literature you're into there."

"Yeah, well, unlike real life, things always seem to work in these," she offered with a shrug. "Besides, she's a favorite author of mine. I found her online about a year ago and I was hooked. But what about you? You don't read?"

She didn't mention the concept, if he said no, was inconceivable to her. Since she'd first learned to read, way back in kindergarten, she'd been a great fan of books.

"I do, but my tastes run more toward Patterson and Cussler, and maybe an occasional Robb." Sliding around a prancing Sarge who was still enjoying the attention Kaylee was giving him, he sat down on the opposite end of the bench.

"Robb, eh?" Tucking the book that had started their comparison of reading material away in her purse, Kaylee sat and scooted around to face him, tucking her hair behind her ear as she did so. "You know that's a pen name, right? A romance writer's alter ego."

"Oh, the horror!" he joked, laughing. He was quick to follow up with, "I did know, actually. Loved her Key series, but you'll never catch me admitting it in public."

Kaylee arched a brow. "Kind of hard to get any more public than this, Parker."

"Ah, but I'm only sharing the truth with you in a *private* conversation, Dean."

"So I can't tell anyone you read romance?" She shook her head and forced her expression into a look of mock disappointment. "What a shame. Cousin Mindy would have a field day with that information. Her latest boyfriend is one of those *women-belong-in-the-kitchen-and-men-only-do-manly-things* types. She would love to have the ammunition in the fight that your confession would provide."

"Fine, fine." He gave in with a put-upon sigh. "You may report your discovery to Cousin Mindy as long as you promise not to utter a peep about me knowing there's a surprise twist near the end of your current read that even I didn't expect."

"What?" Kaylee's brow rose in very real surprise. "Wait. Now even I don't believe you."

"It's true." He raised one hand and stared at his nails with interest. "The guy the heroine's best friend is in love with? She thinks he's a pirate or something equally scandalous, which is why she can never love him. *But ... "*

He leaned close, his eyes sparkling with mischief to conspiratorially whisper, "He's actually a duke!"

Kaylee gasped and her eyes narrowed. "Which is what *she* wants anyway! So why doesn't he tell her?"

Jordan shrugged without bothering to offer more of an explanation, but there was still a brilliant gleam in his eye. Kaylee smacked her palms against her thighs again, but this time in annoyance.

"Blast it! I hate it when the author does stuff like that. There's so much lost time between the sub-characters that can never be made up for." She shook her head in mild disgust with the whole idea, but then a grin slid over her lips. "But wait! That just means there's going to be another book, and now I can hardly wait for more!"

Jordan laughed at her renewed interest and then his expression grew serious. "Never would have pegged you for the romance fiction type, Miss Dean."

"Especially after last night, huh?" Her grin wilted into a wryly twisted smile of self deprecation and she shrugged.

"I wouldn't have believed *you* to be an antiques kind of guy either, Mr. Parker, but we did collide outside of Seville's." Casting him a questioning glance, she said, "You never mentioned what you were looking for that day, or if you managed to find it."

Jordan sat forward on the bench and snapped the lock free on the leash he was holding to allow Sarge a little more freedom before answering. Watching while the retriever bounded off toward the treeline, he shrugged. "A box. Or, *another* box, I suppose I should say. I've quite a growing collection of antique letter boxes, all of them sitting empty throughout the house. Taking up space."

Leaning back again, he shrugged and let his gaze wander across the rather barren winter scenery over her head. "I've been thinking about getting rid of them."

"But—you just bought a new one, right?" Her brow furrowed in confusion. Why he would add a new purchase to a collection he wasn't even going to keep?

Jordan got to his feet. "So I did. Hey, it's daylight. Now would be a great time for you to give me the Hawthorne Grove grand tour. Unless you have to get back to work soon?"

Kaylee wasn't sure why, but she sensed that he was uncomfortable with the subject. Maybe he didn't want anyone questioning his particular interest in antiques? Glancing at her watch, she stood and gathered up her purse and the remnants of her lunch. "I don't have to be at the shelter until three."

"Great!" He whistled for Sarge and started walking and Kaylee fell into step beside him as Sarge ambled up to join them. "That means we have time for some window shopping on the square after the park tour, right?"

"If you want. On the way back, we can stop in at the soda fountain on the corner. Well, it's actually a drug store, but they pull drinks in the back. I'm partial to the Lemon Sour, but I think you'll love their Annihilator."

Jordan winced. "Strange name for a drink."

Shouldering her purse, Kaylee drew the edges of her coat closer to fasten the buttons and laughed. "I agree, but the flavor is to die for, so it's kind of appropriate. You'll see."

He looked doubtful, but by the time they left the shop and headed back to the park, he was in full agreement with her. "This afternoon has been great, Kaylee. Thanks to you, I now know more about Hawthorne Grove's commercial sector than probably three quarters of its residents. Do you even remember how many places we peeked into today? Besides the drug store slash soda shop whose finest attribute is a drink of death." Gesturing toward her with his now empty cup, he said, "I don't think I'll ever forget that one." "We stopped by the Tea Table, which is actually a bed and breakfast that serves high tea, the alternative health store—" Kaylee recounted, counting off each location by holding up a finger.

"Which was aptly dubbed The Herb Garden," Jordan added. "And even though we didn't go there, you did point out the availability of a nightclub, should I acquire an interest in visiting such a rowdy, noisome place—Bonkers, wasn't it?"

"Bollivers," Kaylee corrected with a laugh, ticking off another location on her fingers, "which never opens until after the sun goes down. The owners are a bit eccentric, but their strict after-dark hours still manage to pull in quite a crowd. Then there was Paige's—the bookstore..."

Tipping his head in acknowledgment, Jordan said, "Another brilliantly named establishment, whose owner happens to be *Patrick*, not Paige, as one would assume."

"Oh, and let's not forget—" she started, but he interrupted.

"We even managed to peer discreetly through the darkened windows of the only after hours florist I've ever seen—possibly the only one of its kind in existence, actually—with the also highly appropriate name of Nightshade," Jordan finished for her.

"They have the best flowers, though. My sister, Jo, got me a bouquet from there for my birthday last year and the arrangement lasted for weeks!"

His grin swiftly faded into a serious expression. "I had a really good time today, Kaylee. I'd like to do this again. Well, not *this* precisely, since we've already window shopped all the shops Hawthorne Grove has to offer, but I'm sure we can think of something to do."

Uneasy with the idea of seeing him again—on a regular basis, even, if he meant what she thought he did—she looked away, lowering her eyes. "Jordan, I'd be lying if I said I wasn't flattered because I am, but ... you already know I have no interest in dating again. I'm not on the market for a fling. At all. I had a good time seeing the town with you today, yes, but I don't think I'm up for—"

"For spending an enjoyable day browsing through store windows? Come on, who doesn't love window shopping? And I'm retired, remember? And *bored*, Kaylee. Do you have any idea what it's like for a man who's used to being at the beck and call of an hundred people all day to suddenly find himself with nothing to do?"

He leaned his head back and sighed. "At home, I ramble through my big old empty house all day, wishing I knew someone charming, and fascinating, and yes, someone *fun* to wile away the lonely hours with. Someone who makes me laugh, who loves to surprise me with interesting trivia and tidbits of history, and maybe a little gossip, about this rather eccentric town I've chosen to settle in."

His description made her feel a bit warm and fuzzy inside, but she narrowed her eyes at him and pointed out, "I could name ten people like that, Jordan, right off the top of my head, starting with Cousin Mindy."

Ignoring her sharp look, he lifted his head and asked, "Is she peppy? And quirky? And does she have a cute little dimple at the corner of her mouth that shows up like yours does when she smiles?"

"No, to the dimple, yes to quirky, but I'm not sure about your third requirement." She drew up beside her car and turned to look up at him. "Can you expound upon that one?"

He slid his hands into the deep pockets of his coat and shook his head no. "That's just your coy way of informing me Cousin Mindy doesn't have your cute dimples. I'm sorry, Kaylee, but without dimples, Mindy doesn't fit the bill. It has to be you. No one else possesses the required requisites."

"More like peculiarities," Kaylee pointed out drolly. She tugged her purse around to dig inside for her keys. "We've already seen everything there is to see."

"From the *outside*," he pointed out. "There are worlds awaiting us on the other side of those windows, Kaylee, and I think you know it, too."

His teasing grin was infectious. Kaylee felt her own lips curling in response.

"I can pick a new place each day and spend the afternoon exploring on the inside, but only if you promise you'll come with me."

She continued to give him such a dubious look, he stretched out his hands—which were still snuggled inside the pockets of his coat—making him resemble a giant, swooping bat. "What if I'm shy? I'll never meet anyone without you there to introduce us."

Fighting back a laugh at the comic image of him standing there with his arms outspread like a vampire poised to bite, Kaylee snorted at the absurd notion of him being shy. At the same time, she knew she would enjoy every minute of exploring Hawthorne Grove's quaint little commercial district with him. It would be a rare treat she would honestly hate to miss. But there was that far-too-intimate-for-friends *personal* feel to the whole idea that made her wary.

She peered cautiously up at him. "No strings?"

Leaning close, he lowered his hands and whispered. "No strings."

Then, he leaned forward even more and his lips slid lightly against hers.

She raised her hand to hold him back, to resist, but instead rested her slightly fisted hand against his chest, allowing his warm mouth to linger for a moment before she pushed away, glancing up with a mock accusatory glare to point out that he'd already broken the rules. "You just promised no strings, Jordan, and yet you're ki—"

He kissed her again, more firmly this time, cutting off her admonition.

Her fingers unfolded against his chest and her hand crept upward to the base of his neck; her fingers twisting in the hair at his nape before he broke the kiss and stepped back a half step, a brilliant twinkle in his eyes.

"I said no *strings*, Kaylee Dean, but I never said no kisses."

Chapter Ten

The only way Kaylee could describe the next few weeks of her life was with the word *fun*, but then, a whole host of brilliant, colorful adjectives would swiftly clamor to the fore in her thoughts, and surprisingly, all of them seemed to fit. She hadn't enjoyed herself this much in years—maybe ever—and it was all due to Jordan Parker.

After their day of window shopping on the square, meeting Jordan at lunch to spend a few hours with him before she had to go to the shelter became a regular activity. Some days they merely browsed through the stores on the square, and others they went a little further afield to the malls and boutiques on the more populated side of town, but always, Kaylee enjoyed herself.

Friendly teasing and lots of laughter quickly became the norm, and Kaylee had to admit, even to her friends and family, that yes, she really liked Jordan Parker, even though they weren't actually dating in the traditional sense of the word. They were *friends*.

"Hmm," Jo mused from across a table at Sammy's (which was what Kaylee now called Sam Huntingdon's coffee shop) as she sipped at her steaming brew. "*Friends* don't usually kiss away stray dollops of ice cream from other friends lips, Kaylee, but whatever you say. I won't push it, but only because you seem so different now."

"What do you mean different?"

"Vibrant. Alive. *Happy.*" Jo shifted in her chair to glance toward the back were Jordan was helping Sam put away stock. "He walks into the room and you glow, Kaylee. It's disgusting."

Kaylee couldn't help it. She laughed.

"I glow? Oh, wait. Jordan and I *did* engage in a bit of glow stick tasting recently," she teased. "Must be remnants of the halo green I had."

Jo giggled at that and shook her head. "You see? This is what I mean. Before Jordan came, you never would have joked around about drinking poisonous substances. You'd have been deadly serious if you said anything at all. But now..."

She paused for a moment as if searching for the perfect, non-debatable way to describe the change she saw in Kaylee. "I know both of you have better sense than to actually drink the nasty goop inside a glow stick, Kaylee. I get that you were teasing, and well, that's sort of what I mean."

Leaning forward, she peered at Kaylee, still searching for the words to clarify her thoughts. "Before he showed up it was like you had died inside, you know? You were here and you did your job, you visited with us, with family, when we finally became stern and would no longer accept your thinly disguised excuses, but—you've heard the saying the lights were on but no one was home? Well, in your case, there was a house, but no tenant. You existed, Kaylee, but you were empty inside. You weren't truly living."

"And now I am?"

Settling back in her chair, Jo nodded decisively. "Now you are."

Kaylee shrugged, her fingers busily picking at the corner of the napkin under her cup, and looked away from the seriousness in her sister's eyes. "I didn't think I was so horrible before, Jo, but thank you for letting me know *you* did."

Jo's eyes narrowed. "Not like that, Kaylee. What you're saying isn't what I meant, and you know it. I understood what was going on with you before. We all did. Daniel really hurt you, and it was bad, and I knew the pain of his betrayal would take some time for you to get over. All I am saying now is that —finally, after four long and very dreary years of seeing you hide away and button up the wonderful, loving girl I knew you were inside—I believe you have."

"And you think Jordan is responsible?"

Draining the last swallow of coffee from her mug, Jo stood. "Considering how you were before and how you are now, yes. But if you tell me it's something else, Kaylee, that there's another reason, a better explanation for the sparkle of anticipation in your eyes every time you see him, the glow of happiness that surrounds you when the two of you are together, and the almost youthful bounce in your steps when you hurry to meet him every time he shows up, I promise to try my best to believe you."

"Of course there's a youthful bounce in my steps, Jo. I'm hardly ancient, after all," Kaylee grouched, glaring up at her. "But I'm not so sure Jordan has anything to do with the rest of it."

"You're not certain he's *not*, either, are you?" Jo asked. She tossed some bills and change on the table and tucked her purse under her elbow. "Maybe you should think about it. Think about those meaningless kisses you two share so often and almost indiscriminately these past few days and try to lie to yourself about how much they make you tingle to your toes."

Kaylee gasped at the direction into which their conversation had veered, but Jo only chuckled. "Think about how natural it feels when you melt into his embrace, Kaylee. How comfortable you are when he stands with his arms around you, and how easy it is for you to simply *be* with him."

"Oh, stop it, Jo. Next you'll be telling me I'm curious about the softness of the sheets on his bed."

"Are you?" A wicked smile curved her lips, and she laughed. "You don't need to take it that far, Kaylee. Unless you want to, of course. But I've seen the two of you together, and I've seen you apart, and I have to say you both practically vibrate with awareness when either of you are near the other."

Kaylee shook her head and started to speak, but

Jo waved away her protests. "I've seen it, Kaylee, so don't bother with the denial I know is hovering on your lips. The longer you two are separated, the more whatever this thing is between you intensifies. It's like barely leashed anxiety, just waiting for the moment when you're close again to relax."

Kaylee ignored the blush burning her cheeks. She would not admit she'd thought about Jordan's sheets, or his bed, or his home, or anything other than the enjoyable time they'd spent together during the past few weeks. "You always were the romantic in the family."

"I've always been the *smart* one, too, and if you'll think about it, you'll know I'm right," she teased, heading for the door.

"I'm leaving," she called over her shoulder, and Kaylee looked up to see Jordan standing with his arms crossed over his chest as he leaned against the back wall behind the counter, watching them. Was he really waiting for Jo to leave?

"You can have her back now, Jordan," she finished as she pushed open the door and stepped out. Glancing back through the glass, she saw Jordan start immediately toward Kaylee's table, and a knowing grin curled her lips. At Kaylee, she arched a brow and mouthed a single word. "See?"

Kaylee made a face and waved goodbye to her sister through the window before turning to greet Jordan with a smile. "All finished in the back?"

"Yep." He leaned down for a quick kiss, which she offered naturally, without thought or hesitation.   "Sam can safely offer coffee for another week without worrying his wares will run dry. Are you ready to head out?"

"Let me get my coat." She finished off her mocha latte with a single sip. "Where are we going today? And where's Sarge? I know you had him in the truck earlier."

"Shopping. Dinner. Theater," he said with a shrug. Busy sliding into her coat and slipping on her gloves, she barely noticed he hadn't elaborated. "Not until later, though. It'll be a while before we get there. Sarge is in the back. Sammy promised to keep an eye on him for me until we get home."

"Shopping, dinner, yes, but where? We've been through every place I know in town, Jordan. Some of them more than twice. You can't possibly want to do it all again."

"Hey, you've spoiled me to those Annihilators and Lemon Sours, Kaylee Dean," he said. She felt the warmth of his palm settle near the base of her spine as he ushered her toward the door. "So it's all your fault if I want to keep going back."

"See you Monday, Sammy!" he called out as she pushed open the door.

Monday. Kaylee knew there was something significant about his answer, but she was too curious about where he planned to take her to give her mind time to catch up and figure out what it was. Five minutes later, they were cruising down the highway, the radio humming with the sound of one of the latest pop tunes in the background while they chatted about her morning. Twenty five minutes after that, Kaylee realized they were stopping, that they'd reached their destination, and it was a place she'd never been before.

Jordan parked in front of a large metal building then got out and came around the front of the truck to open the passenger side door. Reaching up, he offered a hand to help her down. Loud, rumbling noises accompanied by a whining whir buffeted her ears and she winced. "Where are we?"

"It's a surprise."

He said the words casually if a little louder than normal, but Kaylee could sense a new tension about him in the way he avoided her eyes every time she asked a question about where they were or where they were going. She frowned. "Jordan ... "

Slipping his hand into hers, he curled their fingers together and tugged her playfully toward the front of the building. "You'll see. Come on, Kaylee. There are at least an hundred things I want you to see today, but if you insist on stalling, we'll be late."

As soon as they walked through the door, Kaylee understood. She pulled back. "An airplane hangar?"

"Private landing strip." Jordan pointed toward another, smaller set of double doors at the back of the building. "Our ride awaits us right through there."

Sensing her hesitation, he paused to peer down at her, doubt and excitement warring for place in his gaze before he forced the plea in them to become earnest. "I want to share something with you, Kaylee. Something I—I can't explain. But I can show you. I *want* to show you and I promise you will enjoy it, but I don't want to go if you're going to feel uncomfortable about it. Will you come with me?"

Brakes, Kaylee thought. She really needed to step on the brakes for this one. *Hard.*

"Jordan, I—there's an airplane out there! I—I can't get on a plane!"

"Are you afraid of flying?" he teased, but when she shook her head and tried to pull her hands out of his, his expression changed to one of genuine concern.

"No, it's not that. It's ..."

Kaylee felt her brow tug downward in a serious frown. How could she explain this to him? Were there even words to describe the mixed tangle of emotions she was suddenly feeling? She'd been okay with spending time with him here in Hawthorne Grove. Hawthorne Grove was home. It was familiar. But now he wanted to take her somewhere new, somewhere that required an airplane trip to see, and she didn't think she was ready for—for *this*. Whatever *this* was.

"How long will we be away?"

"I was hoping for the weekend, but if you want to come back before then, we can."

The weekend? She needed to call her mother. She should call Jo, too, and Mindy. And Marc, just in case they didn't make it back before her shop opened on Monday morning. He could call her appointments and reschedule, and... She shook her head. "I didn't even pack a bag!"

"You won't need it. I did mention shopping, remember?" He squeezed her fingers lightly. "There is nothing to be afraid of, Kaylee. I'll be right beside you the entire time, just as you've been at mine these past few weeks. Well, except for when you're sleeping, but even then I'll be right across the hall. I won't let anything bad happen to you. I promise. Will you come?"

His words were innocent enough, but she knew there was really another unspoken question being asked, one only his eyes revealed; one she was terrified to answer. It was a question of trust, and the last time she had given it, she'd been burned. Badly. But what really stunned and frightened her right now, however, was recognition of her intense desire to say yes, to give in. To tentatively hand over her permission and the keeping of her heart to him...

Jo's conversation in the coffee shop came rushing back and she almost staggered under the blow of realization when it came. Some time during the past weeks, while they were jaunting around town under the guise of friendship, sharing unexpected moments of warmth and laughter and just plain fun, she had begun to enjoy his company. She had relaxed with him, grown comfortable with being by his side and having him at hers, but worse, she realized now, had been getting through the hours while he was away.

Jo was right.

She *already had* let Jordan in and she was suddenly afraid if she agreed to go with him now, she would be getting way over her head into something she could not easily define. She and Jordan were friends, and yet at the same time, she could not deny they were becoming so much more and she needed to decide just how much more she was prepared to allow, and quickly.

Looking up at him, seeing the eager but subdued anticipation and expectancy in his eyes while the thoughts in her head screamed at her to run away, to go home and lock herself in, to hide from the possibility of being forced to drown in a fresh new sea of pain she was scarce prepared to deal with so soon after Daniel, she opened her mouth to refuse. To say no. To ask him to take her home again, where she would be safe.

At the same time, her heart chided her for her fear, pointing out in a way she could not deny that she had never felt more comfortable, more relaxed and secure in her life than she did when she was with Jordan.

"I'll go."

Chapter Eleven

"Well. That was an hundred times easier than I thought it would be," Mortianna said, a note of genuine surprise tinting her voice. "I didn't even get a chance to make her twist an ankle or fall into an unexpected faint!"

"As much as you'd like to believe otherwise, Morty, people can think and make decisions for themselves," Serephina pointed out, smugness clearly evident in her tone. "Kaylee's got a brain in her head, you know."

With the first round of what was sure to become a lengthy and completely pointless argument between her siblings already said and done, Esmerelda surreptitiously stepped between her sisters and their immediate view of the scrying dish.

Glancing down into the shimmering liquid, she almost cringed.

Almost.

Then she remembered her sisters couldn't actually see what was happening with Jordan and

Kaylee at the moment, and she felt a rush of relief, followed immediately by a sense of urgency. If she was seriously going to do *the thing*, this was likely to be her one and only chance.

But—what if they figured it out? What if Serephina—eagle eyed and hyper-sensitive as she was—zoned in on the differences in her stance, her speech, her coloring? Fighting back her anxiousness over the possibility of getting caught, Esmerelda counted to ten, exhaled slowly and lifted her chin, facing her sisters with a slightly calmer sense of determination. "Wait, he's taking Kaylee to the opera, isn't he?"

"Mmm-hmm," Mortianna said, nodding excitedly, a bright smile arching her lips. Giving her shoulders a little shrug, she quivered, ecstatic to see things were going so well between their charges. "It's so *Pretty Woman*, isn't it?"

"One could even say it's so *cliché*," Serephina sarcastically added in response to Mortianna's romanticism while moving around Morty's chair to settle into her favorite corner of the sofa. But Esmerelda noticed she was doing a little smiling of her own.

"Aren't you two forgetting something? Or rather, some*one*?" Peeking furtively at the scene with Kaylee and Jordan still open inside, Esmerelda sidled casually around the scrying dish, hiding it with her body while she did her best to continue to speak casually, pointing out the one glaringly obvious fact both her sisters were missing. "If you'll think about it for a minute, you will remember there's another woman in NYC who will be heading to *the Met* tonight."

Blast it! Her words were too hasty, her tone too high, and she sounded like a twittering magpie!

Biting her tongue, Esmerelda fell silent, holding her breath while she waited, hoping her sisters would make the connection she wanted them to make both quickly and without recalling the scene still revealing the couple in Hawthorne Grove whom they had scryed.

"Stacy!" The name exploded into the room as both her sisters reached the desired conclusion simultaneously. Mortianna's eyes narrowed and she turned a pleading glance in Serephina's direction. "Feeny? How about a little glamour spell? Turn her into a cat, or something? Just for tonight. Please?"

Caught in the act of pulling over the mauve and gold upholstered hassock, Serephina propped her feet on the woven material, crossed her legs at the ankles, and shook her head no—just as Esmerelda had known she would. "We can't. That's breaking the rules."

According to Serephina, everything was breaking the rules. Esmerelda barely restrained herself from rolling her eyes. When it came to people falling in love, there was nothing they could do—nothing *magical* anyway.

After several long minutes of thoughtful silence, Esmerelda could swear she actually physically felt the touch of their gazes when both her sister's eyes slid hopefully in her direction. *Stop it, Ezzi. You're being overly sensitive because of you-know-what.* Forcing herself to breathe normally, she calmly returned their stares.

Mortianna was the one who finally spoke up, daring to ask, "Merry? Any ideas?"

Esmerelda bit her lip. She had a few, but none she felt like sharing—mostly because they had nothing to do with Jordan and Kaylee and the inevitable run-in they would have had with Stacy Blaut later this evening. Feigning disappointment, she shook her head no.

Then, when she was certain the moment was right, she lifted her head and held up a hand to signal for a silent moment of pause while she gathered her thoughts. "Wait. Hold on..."

She cocked her head to the side, then almost nearly ruined the moment by giggling when both her sisters actually nodded, granting permission for her unspoken request to be given a second to compose her thoughts.

For once, Mortianna and Serephina were the ones who waited with bated breath while Esmerelda closed her eyes and pretended to think. It wasn't *really* evil of her—was it?—to keep them in suspense for a moment or two longer than was really necessary before she opened her eyes again and asked, "Why don't we join them?"

Serephina angled her head a bit, her expression still and studious while she pondered the suggestion. Mortianna, who had been sitting as straight and tense as a fence post a moment before, fell back into her chair, her expression positively rapturous. Her pleasure daze was fleeting, however. Her eyes flew open and she sat up, her fingers clutching at the edge of the wooden table Serephina often used for a desk.

"*Us* go to New York? Yes! It's brilliant, Merry! Oh, the shopping and the—the shopping!" She practically bounded out of her chair. "I have to pack. I don't even know what to pack! Can you believe it? I can't even remember the last time I—"

Catching a glance of her older sibling out of the corner of her eye, her words broke off suddenly. If anyone would need to be convinced, Mortianna knew exactly who it would be. She turned to look at her sister. "Feeny?"

"Serephina, think about it, really. What would it hurt?" Esmerelda added, quickly pointing out, "If we were there, we could keep a closer eye on things, create a distraction if necessary. A mortal, non-rule breaking one."

"Yes, I'm even willing to promise *no magic*," Mortianna agreed, still practically bouncing on her toes with excitement. When Serephina turned her doubtful gaze on her but declined to comment, Mortianna didn't actually squirm, but she did try a different tact. "You have to admit the last thing we need at this point is for Kaylee and Jordan to run into Miss Blaut."

Esmerelda nodded, adding her own thoughts to Mortianna's. "Kaylee's finally comfortable with him. I believe she's coming around, but—can you even imagine how much a run in with Jordan's ex-girlfriend would set us back?"

"Weeks. Maybe even months, Serephina," her sister answered.

Grateful beyond explanation for Mortianna's quick thinking, relief once again rushed over Esmerelda in waves. "With our current schedule being what it is, I don't think we could handle a set-back like that. Not now."

Especially not now.

There were simply too many things in the works, too many heart strings being tugged and twined and weaved and twisted to let this particular strand become unraveled. Although she was fairly certain Serephina was already on the verge of agreeing, Esmerelda couldn't resist giving an extra nudge, one she knew was guaranteed to win her over. "The CHG would be on us in a flash."

"Oh, that's the last thing we need," Serephina blurted, covering her face with her hands while Mortianna reacted by clapping her hands and jumping up and down in a child-like display of exuberance.

"We're going to New York!" Morty squealed while doing a little eyes-closed kind of happy dance in her seat.

Biting at the inside of her cheek to keep from grinning like a novice with her first willow branch over her success, Esmerelda sprang into action. "I'll put this stuff away and you two can start packing."

Mortianna was two thirds of the way up the winding, spiral stairs with Serephina only a few steps behind her when Serephina paused, turning back to Esmerelda. "Oh, wait. We can't—the quilt, remember? The female half of our next assignment will be here before noon tomorrow. We can't leave without—"

Looking down at her sister with a slight scowl marring her brow, Mortianna dropped back against the wall and grumped, "Why can't we use the replication spell? There's never been a bigger need for us to be in two places at once!"

At the foot of the stairs, Esmerelda froze. Her shoulders drooping with disappointment. "I forgot about the quilt."

How was she to get around this one? Counting to three, she forced herself to focus on the problem at hand and think. It didn't help, so she continued. She'd barely reached the count of nine when her head popped up again. "Mortianna can stay."

"Me?" her sister whined. "Why does it have to be me?"

Stamping her feet on the stairs, Mortianna said, "No, no, no! Feeny can stay. She doesn't even *like* the opera!"

"True," Serephina agreed. "But I happen to love making sure our charges don't get derailed, that we don't receive unwanted visits from the CHG, and the idea of staying here while leaving things in the Big Apple in *your* hands almost terrifies me."

"I suppose *I* could stay," Esmerelda offered before their back-and-forth argument could gather steam. "That way you could go with Mortianna, to make sure she doesn't get her witchy fingers into anything unsavory, and I can meet our newest assignee."

"Oh, but you'll miss *everything*, Merry, and it's been so long!" Mortianna protested.

Esmerelda shrugged. "I don't see any other way, Morty. Either I stay, or we all stay, and in the case of the latter, we would be doing so knowing we run the risk of … "

"Botching one assignment to fulfill another." This came from Serephina, who turned to her with an expression of uncertainty and concern. "Are you sure you don't mind staying behind, Merry?"

"Of course I mind, but there's really nothing else we can do." She shrugged for added effect, and then waved away Serephina's concern with a smile. "I'll be fine. There's always going to be a New York and there will be another day, another chance for me to see the sights. Now is your turn. Yours and Mortianna's."

With a flick of her wrists and a few waves of her hands, she urged her sisters up the stairs to their rooms. "Go. Enjoy it. Have fun—lots of it! When you get back here, you can tell me all about it and I'm sure I'll feel as if I had gone with you myself."

* * *

Back at the private landing strip, Jordan wavered in indecision. Although Kaylee had agreed to the trip, he could sense her reluctance, and the anxiety she felt over her decision to go with him was clear in her eyes. He had been looking forward to this for days now, but biting back a sigh, he almost called the whole thing off.

The past few weeks he'd spent with Kaylee had been some of the most enjoyable of his life. They had become friends and maybe a little more, and it was the *little more* was what worried him when he saw the uncertainty in her eyes. He didn't want to ruin this fragile new thing he could sense growing between them by forcing her to deal with issues she obviously wasn't ready to face.

Not that he had anything illicit planned. He only wanted to take her to see the opera. But looking at her now, he was having second thoughts. "Are you sure? I wouldn't want you to feel—"

A vibration interrupted, signaling an incoming call on his cell, and he sighed. "One second."

Palming his phone, he glanced at the screen and frowned. Sammy? His thoughts immediately went to Sarge, and he answered the call. "Sam? Hi. Everything okay?"

"You aren't on the plane yet, are you?" Sam asked, and Jordan tensed, unreasonably expecting the worst.

"No, not yet. I'd barely managed to convince Kaylee to come along with me before you called and we were just about to head out. What's up?"

"Well, I hate to say it but it's less a *what* and more a *who*, but as long as you're still on the ground, I think it's safe to say you might want to delay your flight so you can take care of this one personally, man. You've got company."

Company?

Some days Sam's penchant for being vague was

irritating and today just happened to be one of those days. "Sammy, you're being about as clear as mud again. Explain, please and—keep it brief? I've got a plane to catch, remember?"

"Uh, yeah. Okay. Two words. Stacy Blaut. On your doorstep. With bags. Oh, wait, that was seven, but I'm guessing the first two would have been enough. Am I right?"

"Stacy? What would—why?"

Jordan closed his eyes. With Stacy, there didn't have to be a reason. There were so many things she did simply because she believed she could. He wouldn't put it past her having decided an extended stay in the country was just what she needed, and so she'd driven down to his place for the duration. It would never have occurred to her that he might be unavailable to put her up for it, or rather, she would pretend it hadn't, and he didn't want to cause an uproar so soon after coming to Hawthorne Grove by calling the cops to have them escort her off the property.

Resigned now to canceling the flight and annoyed because he would rather have done so for almost any other reason, he sighed into the phone. "I'll be there. Give me half an hour."

Ending the call, he turned back to Kaylee. "Will you be disappointed if I ask for a rain check?"

Kaylee shook her head yes, but said, "Not at all."

He wasn't surprised, but neither was he particularly eager to answer the questions he could see burning in her gaze. Rather than put her off, he simply didn't give her time to ask them. "I have to speak with Hank, let him know we won't be flying out today after all, but it'll only take a minute. Wait for me in the truck?"

"Sure."

He handed her the keys. "It's probably still warm inside, but take these, just in case. I'll explain on the way home."

Chapter Twelve

Home.

There was that word again—a peculiarly deceptive word that meant different things to different people, Kaylee thought as Jordan walked away. Its definition could change depending upon where one was in the overall course of their lives and one's experiences seemed to play a fine hand in the shaping of their individual sense of meaning for the word.

At the moment, Kaylee's current understanding of it was giving her very mixed feels because, for her, home was more than simply the roof under which one lived. At this particular time in her life, where she lived was the small, one bedroom apartment in town that served as her sanctuary—a place to rest, from work and from her daily interactions with the outside world.

She'd been so proud of herself when she'd moved in.

The apartment served as a symbol of her success and independence—but it wasn't *home*.

Jo teasingly referred to it as the Hideout occasionally—a place of quiet solitude to which Kaylee retreated—sometimes for days—when the pain of her past would rise up to haunt her in the present. But Jo never let her remain shut up inside for too long. Deans didn't hide, Jo would gently remind her, and Kaylee would feel immediately obligated to prove her right because, as her older, smarter, and wiser sister, Jo Dean Leavy was never wrong.

Mindy called it the Halfway House because it was the one place she knew she could crash when school, her friends, her parents, and her sometimes hectic social schedule made her feel half crazy and she needed a break from it all.

Marc called it the Lecture Hall because every time he stopped by, the two of them fell into lengthy philosophical and oftentimes highly intellectual debates about life in general, and occasionally, to Kaylee's profound annoyance, *her* life in particular. Or more specifically, all the things missing from it.

A wry smile pulled at her lips. Marc believed all the good things in life revolved around having someone to share it with. There had been a time when Kaylee would have wholeheartedly agreed, but now she tended to be more careful with whom she shared bits of herself.

Until Jordan...

Out of nowhere, he'd dropped into her life. From their very first meeting, he'd made an indelible impression on her. By their third, she had already become accustomed to his presence in her thoughts, and every happy, fun-filled, pleasurable moment she had spent in his company since had only strengthened her acceptance of him in her world.

But to go *home with* Jordan ...

Suddenly, the word took on a whole new world of meaning. In this case, home was different somehow. Home meant more—a *lot* more—than just the place where he lived, and Kaylee was finding the word surprisingly difficult to define. She simply knew her apartment wasn't it.

Somewhere in the hangar, a door slammed shut with a loud bang, startling her out of her musings. She blinked and then shivered. Casting a quick glance through the wide window at an overly bright sky that hinted of coming snow, she pulled her coat closer and headed for the exit, her thoughts preoccupied once more with the idea of going home with Jordan.

Clutching his keys tightly against her palm as she pushed through the double doors back into the chilly air outside, she tried to ignore the crazy cozy feelings suddenly warming her insides that she got from thinking about it.

Despite having spent the better part of the past few weeks at his side, she had yet to invite him back to her apartment, or to venture out with him to see where *he* lived. Not that he'd asked, but thinking about it shouldn't have felt any different than when she'd agreed to fly off to wherever with him in his private jet. And yet, it did. Vastly so.

A trip meant impersonal hotels with completely separate rooms, but *home* ...

A thrill of anticipation and excitement zinged through her, tempered only by the stinging prickle of warning at the back of her mind that suggested riding out to Jordan's place—no matter how innocent such a visit might seem on the surface—could become insidious in a heartbeat.

Going home with him would make everything more intimate. More personal. It would change things between them. It would change *her*, irrevocably so, and she wasn't sure she was willing to take the risk.

Her earlier conversation with Jo came to mind, forcing her to think, to examine her thoughts and re-examine her feelings where Jordan was concerned. She needed to step back and take a look at everything that had happened since the day she'd met him outside Seville's Antiques and Collectibles and to decide—here and now—what was really happening between them.

Sure, they were more comfortable and relaxed with each other now. Spending several hours of every day in the company of anyone who was as easy to be with as Jordan was made it kind of impossible to remain aloof. She could not have done it if she had tried, but she hadn't tried because Jordan really hadn't given her the chance.

Without an ounce of charm, superficial or otherwise, he'd stumbled up against her life and with the light of challenge gleaming in the depths of his intriguing gray eyes. He'd coaxed her into allowing him inside. With confident sincerity, he'd promised to keep things light between them and then surprised her when she'd cracked with his gentle acceptance and understanding.

His curiosity and genuine interest in everything she could possibly show him was contagious. Who could have thought it possible to discover so much about the town where she'd lived her entire life in just the few short weeks she'd spent at his side?

Somehow, Jordan Parker made the mundane come alive, changing an everyday shopping spree into a fun-filled adventure into the unknown. His frequent spontaneity was exciting and his kisses provocative. In his arms she always felt warm and safe, and though the touch of his lips on hers often hinted at a smoldering, underlying passion that could be very satisfying to explore if only she would give it a try, so far he'd kept his word about no pressure and no strings.

There was no doubt about it—Kaylee had thoroughly enjoyed every moment she spent with him. But was it possible she'd enjoyed some of them more than she should?

It was easy to admit they were becoming friends, but...was there something else? Something more meaningful and infinitely more dangerous to her heart beginning to grow between the two of them?

Shivering now from the cold, Kaylee ducked her head against a particularly biting burst of wind and pressed forward the last few steps to the truck. Dancing from one foot to the other to ward off the chill seeping beneath the folds of her coat, she clicked the button on the thingy on Jordan's key ring to unlock the door and opened the one on the passenger side to climb in, her thoughts still caught by the unsettling realization that she might be falling in love again.

How could such a thing have happened without her being aware of what was going on? There would have been clues. Hints to warn her things between her and Jordan were slipping into a territory she wasn't ready to re-explore. Maybe the signs had been there all along but she'd been enjoying herself so much she'd simply refused to let herself see?

Lost in thought, she jumped when the driver side door popped open and Jordan slid in behind the wheel, rapidly rubbing his bare hands together to ward off the cold.

Both hands on her chest now, she swung her head to stare at him wide-eyed. "Good grief, you startled me!"

"Sorry, it's frigid in here!" He continued to rub at his hands while his gaze flitted from the empty ignition switch, to the dash, and then to the seat before finally rising to settle on her, his brow wrinkled by a slight frown of confusion. "I gave you the keys, didn't I?"

"What? I—yes, you did. Sorry. I was preoccupied."

She handed over the keys and he started the engine, then cranked up the heat. "It's getting colder out there. Hank said it looks like their might be snow."

At the mention of snow, her thoughts drifted to the beautiful snow globe she'd bought at Seville's the day she'd first met him, and she thought of the house inside, her mind suddenly making clear to her the definition of the word home.

Home meant comfort and security.

Home meant freedom to be who you were—the real you—and still find acceptance.

Home meant a never-ending supply of concern and understanding and sensitivity.

And home meant special memories—the kind that either grounded you or sent your spirits soaring.

In a word, home was not a place at all, but rather, a feeling—the word, in fact, embodied the highest emotion of all. Home, Kaylee realized at last, meant "anywhere you feel loved."

Just as she had suspected, it had nothing to do with the structure in which one lived but everything to do with the people who resided inside and the certain knowledge was almost terrifying. But worse than having come to a full understanding of what home truly meant to her was the uncomfortable yet undeniable truth which followed: Jordan had become home for her.

Wherever he was, as long as she was at his side, she felt completely at ease and at home—and that frightened her.

"I'm sorry I had to cancel our trip." Jordan said, glancing over while backing carefully out of the parking space. "I was really looking forward to showing you the city. Kind of like repaying the favor you've granted me—helping me get familiar with the sights and sounds of Hawthorne Grove."

"It's not a problem," she absently assured him, her entire being still reeling from reaction to her discovery. "In fact, it's probably for the best that we didn't go."

There was a little quaver in her voice there at the end. Closing her eyes, she turned quickly away toward the window, hoping he hadn't noticed the betraying little catch of sound that heralded an imminent onset of tears, but when she cast a quick glance over at him she saw a confused frown knitting his brow yet again.

"Hey, are you okay?"

Not trusting her voice to not crack if she spoke, Kaylee nodded instead in answer to his question. But the truth was, she wasn't sure. *Was* she okay? Or had she let this thing with Jordan go too far? The recent realizations she had made clearly said she had—if her intention was to protect her heart from danger of breaking. "I'm fine, but I think I'd rather you drop me back at Sam's, if you don't mind."

He cast her another quick glance as he maneuvered off the little side road onto the highway. This time, his eyes were filled with more than confusion, but Kaylee could not seem to make herself hold his gaze long enough to sort through the myriad questions she saw there. She'd already dealt with more emotion than she cared to today. Right now, all she wanted to do was get back to her apartment where she could figure out how to deal with the startling revelation she had uncovered.

"Alright. It's probably a good idea that you don't meet Stacy yet, anyway. She can be a bit ... difficult at times."

Kaylee felt her brow pull downward, just now realizing there was a decided significance in the way he said the name, one she didn't yet understand, but had a feeling she should. Her head swung round, her gaze flying up to meet his. "Stacy?"

Jordan's shoulder rose and fell in a halfhearted, nonchalant shrug. "My ex. Apparently, she's camped out on my doorstep and I need to find out why."

His ex? Ex-girlfriend? Or ex-*wife*?

In either case, Kaylee's reaction was decidedly not good and she expected any attempts at an explanation he might make would only produce more of the same breathless fear of impending destruction. Clutching her hands in her lap, she quietly reminded herself to breathe while dread poured over her in icy sheets, chilling the blood in her veins. "Camped out?"

His gaze focused on the road, Jordan nodded. "Yep. Sam said it looked like she planned to stay for a while."

He offered the words so calmly it frightened her. But when he didn't deny that she would, indeed, be spending some time with him, Kaylee squeezed her eyes closed, fighting against the blindingly obvious demonstration of his betrayal, a swiftly rising sense of panic, and the terribly familiar crushing weight of inexplicably harrowing pain.

She could feel the color leeching from her as surely as she felt the sting of bile rising in her throat. Turning toward the window again, she put her hands over her face this time, hoping that maybe he wouldn't notice she'd gone pale.

How could this be happening to her—again?

Eyes burning with the sting of unshed tears and her throat tight against the thick swell of emotions pouring through her, Kaylee slid one hand toward the button to lower her window. Her fingers trembled and she seriously needed some air. The glass lowered and she turned her face into the frigid wind, sucking in several quick, deep breaths.

"Kaylee? Are you sure you're okay? You've been so quiet today—"

She could hear his voice. She understood his question. She even recognized the genuine sound of concern in his voice, but at the moment, her very newly mended heart was breaking again and none of it mattered. Somehow she managed to shake her head yes, to deter both his questions and his concern, but her stomach still rolled.

Turning away to stare out the window again, she squeezed her fists into tight balls in her lap, willing away the nausea in her gut. If they could just make it back to Sammy's, everything would be alright. She could get into her own car and drive back to the sanctuary of her apartment and think. But they were still driving and Sammy's felt a world away, and...and she was pretty sure she'd fallen head over heels in love with Jordan H. Parker.

Oh, no. I think I'm going to be sick.

Chapter Thirteen

Jordan thought he should have felt something when he saw Stacy again for the first time since their breakup, but other than an eagerness to see the last of her once he found out why she had come, there was nothing.

"Hello, Jordan. It's been a while," she said, a hesitant smile touching her lips. "How have you been?"

Jordan motioned for Sarge to jump down then closed the truck door and, crossing his arms over his chest, he leaned back against the fender and eyed her suspiciously. "Better than when I left the city. How about yourself? What are you doing here, Stacy? Sam said you arrived with luggage."

His words seemed to spark a reminder. "Oh, that! Yes, I did. Was that him in the black Durango? I thought it was you, that I'd just missed you."

Walking to her car, she opened the back and reached inside. "I was digging in my bags for this."

The door closed again and she walked up to him, holding out a package with wrinkled wrapping paper on the outside. "It's a little worse for wear, but—this is for you. Open it."

Warily, he did. Inside was a letter box. He lifted the lid. There was a folded note lying in the bottom. He flicked it open with one finger. A single word was written on the paper inside. It said, "Sorry."

"Okay. What does this mean, Stacy? You know I don't like games."

"No game." She was shaking her head. "It's a sincere apology. One I needed to make before I said thank you—for throwing me out of your life and making me see the light."

"I'm seeing someone," he said quickly, before she could launch into some spiel about how she missed him and wanted to be with him again, but she surprised him by laughing instead.

"Me, too! His name is Weston McKinley, and we are getting married." Leaning close, she whispered, "I'm marrying *someone else*, Jordan, so you can relax."

His expression must have revealed just how stunned he was by her announcement because she laughed. "That's why I came—to invite you to the wedding. Well, firstly to apologize, and then to issue the invitation, but—you will come, won't you?"

"Married." Jordan dropped the word like a rock and shook his head to clear it, totally ignoring the half-hopeful, half-doubtful look in her eyes for the moment. Stacy Blaut was getting married. "Do you love him? Does he love you?"

He didn't know why he was asking, but he felt like he should.

This time when she smiled, her eyes lit in a way he had not seen them do in a long, long time. "Yes! Yes, I do. *We* do! Isn't it crazy?"

Spinning about on her toes, she raised her hands to the sky and declared, "He loves me! Weston Jade McKinley loves me, and he wants me to be his bride!"

Settling down somewhat though the smile curving her ever-glossed lips stayed firmly in place, she said, "And that's why I want you to be there, Jordan. I—I want you to give me away. Will you? Please?"

If he thought he'd been shocked before, now even stunned wouldn't cover his reaction. "Me? I can't give you away, Stacy. Your family..."

"Father is the only member of my family I would have wanted to do the honors, Jordan, but he isn't with us anymore. He would have liked Wes. Don't you think he would have? Oh, wait, you haven't met him yet!"

Her quick, short burst of a laugh was his only indication the subject of who would give her away at her impending wedding was a touchy one for her. "I haven't, true, so I couldn't say, Stace, but what about Nathaniel and Eric? Won't your brothers expect to be the ones to..."

"Eric is standing with Wes as his best man. And you know Nate. He's rarely home and when he is, he doesn't much care what the rest of us are up to."

Her gaze fell. She studied her nails and Jordan fought back the teensiest twinge of guilt for denying her. But, damn it, she was the one who had made things impossible between the two of them. Not that he regretted their split. If anything, seeing her today made him even more grateful that he'd ended things when he had. But even he wasn't so callous he couldn't see this whole wedding thing was important to her. That, in itself, was a revelation to how much she'd changed.

"What about Stanley? I'm sure he'd—"

"Didn't you hear? Uncle Stanley had a heart attack, Jordan. A month after you sent me packing, I got the call. He died in the ambulance on the way to the hospital."

Now he really felt like a douche. "I'm sorry. I hadn't heard."

"Say you'll do it, Jordan. I know you still—still have bad feelings toward me because of our past, but—I really need you to do this. Not because of how we were or what we hoped we might become, but because you're the only person who's ever really made a difference in my life since Father died."

Jordan snorted at her skewed sense of logic. "I kicked you out of our apartment. How is that classified as making a difference?"

"I don't know how to explain it, Jordan, but it did." She shrugged. "Really."

She cocked her head to the side and stood staring up at the big Hawthorne tree in his yard in silence for a moment. "It was like, until the day you asked me to leave, I was blind, you know? Maybe it sounds silly, but even though I knew we were together, that I was as much an adult as you and just as responsible and capable of doing my part to make things work between us, I couldn't really *see* that I wasn't.

"Your decision to end things between us was a gift, Jordan. Like sight to a blind man. For the first time in my life, I realized it was time I stopped relying on others for my happiness and to go out and make my own."

Her eyes, when she looked at him again, were shiny with a fine misting of tears. "And I did it. I took responsibility for my own life, for my own happiness, and that is when I found Wes. Or, more accurately, that is when Wes found me."

Two steps put her squarely in front of him. She looked up with a smile and said, "I'm happy now, Jordan. Really, truly happy for the first time in my life, and I have you to thank for it."

Jordan knew when he was beaten, and now was a perfect example of it. He closed his eyes, took a deep breath, and said, "Fine, I'll do it. Unless Nate steps up, and he might, Stacy."

"You will? Oh, thank you!" Squealing her happiness, Stacy stood on her toes and hugged him. "This is wonderful, Jordan! You're the best!"

"Unless Nate decides to do the right thing, as your oldest brother. And you have to promise me if he does, you will let him. Deal?"

She grinned and reached out a hand to shake on it. "Deal."

* * *

Across town, Kaylee grabbed a spoon for her yogurt from the kitchen and headed to the small, afghan covered sofa that nestled beneath the one big window in her living room. Tucking her feet beneath her, she ducked her head over the yogurt cup and dug in, ignoring the piercing look her sister slanted her way.

"Did you even bother to ask him?" Jo asked. "I think if things had gone far enough between Michael and I for me to agree to go away for the weekend with him, I'd have asked if he was married the minute he mentioned an ex."

"Of course I didn't, Jo. Why would I? He said she was *waiting* for him. He said she was going to *stay*. I didn't see any reason to ask questions, since the answers were obviously none of my business."

Jo shot a glance heavenward and rolled her eyes. "No, there you're wrong. You've spent the past several weeks with him under the impression he was available. If he gave the wrong impression, you have a right to know. Call him. I know he's been calling you."

"How do you know that?" Kaylee asked around the tip of her spoon.

Jo snorted. "You look at your phone every time it vibrates. If it were Mom, or Min, or any one of a dozen other people you'd have answered it by now, if only to avoid talking to me. So it's Jordan. Six times now, if my count isn't off. See what he wants,

Kaylee. Return his call."

She held Kaylee's phone out to her but Kaylee shook her head, ignoring the offering. "I can't."

"Why not? Look, either something happened between you and Jordan today or something should have. Which is it?"

"He asked me to go away with him for the weekend."

"We've already established that, Kaylee. And you told him you would go. But now you're here, sucking down yogurt as if there won't be any tomorrow and I can tell you've been crying. So his ex showed up. So she planned to stay. That doesn't mean Jordan is going to let her."

"Maybe," Kaylee mumbled around another mouthful of yogurt. "But maybe I just don't care, okay?"

Jo's eyes widened. "Don't care? Oh, don't even try to go there with me, Kaylee Dean. I know better. And I think you've assessed the situation wrongly this time. Jordan likes you. A lot. He may even love you. In fact, I am pretty darn sure he does love you. And I don't think he's going to let this ex, whoever she is, spoil the good thing he's had going with you now that she's here."

Still holding Kaylee's cell phone, she stepped across her sister's feet and plopped down on the sofa beside her. "Have a little faith, won't you? Sometime or another you've got to realize every man in the world is not Daniel and it might as well be now."

The peal of her doorbell roused Jo from her seat.

Making a face at Kaylee as she passed, she pulled open the door without bothering to ask who was on the other side—and turned back to her sister with a snarky expression and a teasing little smile twisting her lips. "Well, speak of the devil and the devil appears. Kaylee, it's Jordan. Should I let him in?"

Kaylee nodded and Jo stepped aside to allow her unexpected visitor access to the apartment. "Mr. Parker. What are you doing here? I thought you had company."

"I came to see you, Miss Dean, and I thought we were well past the formal use of last names only."

Jo snorted. "She just wants to know if you're married—or if you've been married. Are you? Have you? Nosy older sisters want to know."

"No, and no, but why would you think I was married?"

"Your company."

"That's enough, Jo. I think I can speak for myself."

"Now that I've broken the ice anyway." She shrugged. "Michael is expecting me. He texted me at Huntingdon's and I told him I'd come to check on Kaylee but that I'd be home soon. Y'all have fun now, ya hear?"

Kaylee glared while she shouldered her purse and let herself out, then turned to Jordan. "She's such a pest."

Jordan cocked a brow. "If you were curious about my visitor, Kaylee, why didn't you just ask me?"

"I didn't think I had a right to dig into your personal life."

Both brows rose. "My—I don't have a personal life, Kaylee. Not yet. No, at the moment, my one relationship is very, very public."

Kaylee's narrowed eyes held his. "Are you talking about me, Jordan? About us? Because that's really what I need to know. If there even is an us..."

Jordan held up a hand, then dug into his coat pocket to extract three cases. Movie rentals. All romantic comedy—one specifically the movie she had seen with him when they'd first met. "I hope there is an us, because watching these movies certainly won't be done by me if I have to do it alone. I tried to call, but when you didn't answer, I decided to take a chance and just drop by." His gaze roamed around her combination living/dining/kitchen and he nodded. "Nice. You decorate this yourself?"

"Yes, but I don't understand. You came here to watch a movie?"

"You aren't that dense, Kaylee Dean, so stop trying to break this down and over-analyze it. I had to cancel our trip, but I still want to be with you. So, after my visitor left—and yes, she is gone—I came into town and stopped off at the video rental store for these. I was hoping you'd be here, that you'd be alone, so I could ask you to come home with me instead of flying to New York with me. There won't be a visit to the Metropolitan Opera House, but I can promise dinner and a movie."

"Who is she, Jordan?"

"Stacy? The ex-girlfriend I think I mentioned before. If not, you may assume it was because she isn't that important to me and you will have assumed correctly."

"Why did she come here?"

"Surprisingly enough, to invite me to her wedding. She is getting married next month, and she has asked me to give her away."

"Wow."

"That was my thought, as well, given how things were when I ended it between us, but she's genuinely happy and since her father is gone and her brother is kind of an ass..." He shrugged. "I agreed to do the deed—like any good friend would."

He stepped close and tilted up her chin. "That's all she is, Kaylee. A friend. I'm hoping her brother, Nate, comes around and does the right thing by giving her away himself, but if he doesn't, I didn't think walking her down the aisle to be married to another man would be a problem."

"I suppose it isn't." She could feel a blush burning her cheeks. "Seems kind of silly now."

"What, that you were jealous?" he teased and she flushed hotter.

"I am not jealous. I'd have to care an awful lot to be jealous."

"There is one sure-fire way to make sure I'm not spending my time with another woman, you know. For this weekend, anyway."

"Oh, and that is?"

"Come home with me, Kaylee. Come out to my

place, have dinner, and watch a movie or two. I'll cook. You can sleep in the spare bedroom, if you decide to stay the night, and you should because it'll probably be late when the show is over, but no strings, remember?"

"No strings. Right."

"Not a one—until you're ready. Then, I will be more than happy to tie you into so many knots you'll never find your way free of me, Miss Kaylee-who-lies-badly-about-not-being-jealous-Dean."

Kaylee chuckled. "Fine, fine. I'll come with. Just let me grab a few things, okay?"

She started to turn away, but he grabbed her hands, forcing her to look up at him again.

"Thank you, Kaylee. And for the record, if a guy had showed up at your place, I would be jealous, too."

She was speechless. Was this Jordan's way of telling her he cared about her? Maybe even that he loved her? She didn't know what to say—and then, she didn't have to because someone was knocking at her front door.

"Don't go away. I need to analyze that," she said before hurrying to answer the door. She pulled it open, half expecting Jo to be outside, waiting to tell her "I told you so" but it was not her sister who waited outside her door.

"Hello, Kaylee."

Four years of badness hit her in the gut like a sucker punch from nowhere. "Daniel. What are you doing here?"

Chapter Fourteen

Of all the "he'll be back" scenarios Kaylee had gone through during the four years since Daniel had left Hawthorne Grove, this was the only one that didn't fit. Shocked and confused by his sudden, unexpected reappearance, she stared at him in silence while her mind raced to make quick sense of the moment.

It failed, leaving her momentarily at a loss.

From beneath the bright glare of the pair of outdoor lights illuminating her front stoop, Daniel Sutton, one of her best friends through high-school and the one-time love of her life stared back, and she realized, almost as an afterthought, that she felt strangely unaffected by his presence.

The realization threw her. Wasn't she supposed to be reeling with remembered pain? Or, at the very least, filled with fury and righteous indignation over how and why he had left her? Kaylee raised her hands to her temples in an attempt to stop the whir of thought spinning in her head. She knew she should say something, but the only words that came to mind was the question she had already asked. "What are you doing here?"

With the same hint of a smile lurking just below the surface of an actual reaction ghosting his lips—the kind of smile-not smile she remembered that was as much a part of him as his sun-bleached blond hair, Daniel winked playfully and said, "Looking up old friends. *Special* friends."

The husky intonation he had given the word *special* made Kaylee's gut twist. Special? She wondered if by that he meant *sucker*, as in the kind of woman who fell for the same jerk twice—and got burned both times—because if that was his definition of special, well, special she definitely was not.

He continued to stand in her doorway, his eyes hungrily roaming over her body as if he were a starving man and she was his next meal. Four years ago, a look like that might have made her feel wanted, but right now it was creating another kind of feeling—one that left a bad taste in her mouth.

"It's been a long time, right?"

"Four years," Kaylee said, and he nodded his head while his gaze continued to roam over her, from her hair to her toes and back again.

"You're looking beautiful, as always. You do something to your hair?" He reached toward her to flick his fingers at a loose lock and Kaylee pulled back, but he didn't seem to notice. Instead, he grinned and nodded. "I like it. I like it a lot."

Kaylee said nothing. In fact, she was silent for so long, he finally leaned sideways to peer around her into her sanctuary. "So, can I come in? I feel kind of silly standing out here in the cold."

Kaylee opened her mouth to say all those things she had rehearsed in her mind over the past four years but another deeper, harder voice came from behind, cutting off her words. "We were just on our way out."

Jordan had quietly moved up behind her and when his voice suddenly filled the space of awkward silence, Kaylee almost jumped out of her skin. She hadn't forgotten he was there, exactly. She just hadn't expected him to say anything. But now that he had—and since his hands were now resting solidly at her waist, as if he had stepped up solely to lend her his strength, to keep her upright and steady in this strange moment of emotional paralysis—she melted backward into the safe haven of comfort that was his embrace.

The quick flare of surprise in Daniel's eyes was almost enough to make up for the pain of his leaving four years ago. Tilting her head slightly to stare up at Jordan, she said, "Yes, we were." Glancing back toward her unexpected and unwanted guest who continued to hover in her doorway, she said, "I'm sorry, Daniel. Maybe some other time?"

"Of course," he muttered, but still made no move to go. "Maybe tomorrow after lunch, huh? Coffee at Huntingdon's? I'll even pick you up at the shelter."

"Tomorrow's Saturday," Jordan interrupted. He lifted one hand to her shoulder, letting his thumb caress the sensitive skin below her ear. She stopped herself just short of cuddling into his caress and purring like a cat. What was he doing, petting her like this? And in front of Daniel, too!

"Kaylee doesn't work Saturdays," he said it like a reminder, his tone inferring her schedule was something Kaylee's *special friends* would have known. "But she won't be free for coffee regardless, I'm afraid. Kaylee and I have prior plans—for the entire weekend and pretty much most of the foreseeable future."

Most of the foreseeable future? She glanced back at Jordan, wondering what he was playing at.

He reached over from behind her to collect Kaylee's purse from the table beside the door and then her coat, which he held for her while she slid her arms inside.

Kaylee could see Daniel's irritation with Jordan's presence and solicitous actions rising, but for the moment she kept quiet, happy to let Jordan continue to handle the conversation while she buttoned up the buttons on her swing coat and slid on her gloves.

"I see. And who are you, exactly? I don't remember seeing you around here before."

She had just found the words to tell Daniel in no uncertain terms that he'd have to leave when Jordan put his hand at the small of her back and his lips at her temple, giving her a quick kiss there before following up with gentle little push toward the door. "You go on ahead, sweetheart. I'll get the lights and lock up."

Her brows rose at his pretended familiarity but there was a warning light in his eyes she found she could not ignore. Nodding her agreement, she slid past Daniel and started for the stairs. She had only gone a few steps past the door when she heard Jordan say, "Sorry for the lack of introduction, old man, but Kaylee has a way of making me forget everyone but her."

There was a pause, during which Kaylee imagined Jordan extending his hand. Did Daniel take it? She wondered. Then Jordan said, "Maybe I'd be easier to recognize if you were looking at the cover of *Forbes*? The name's Parker. Jordan Parker. IT billionaire? CTS Enterprises? Former CEO...recently retired, of course," she heard him add the last with a pretense of humility touching his tone. "I moved to Hawthorne Grove about six months ago. And you are?"

Kaylee didn't have to guess what would happen when Daniel realized Jordan really was who he said he was. She could almost imagine the stupefied look on his face when he connected the dots of her past with why she hadn't welcomed him home with open arms and the kiss he obviously wanted. *He'd left her and she landed a billionaire.*

She almost laughed out loud at the thought of it, and probably would have, if she hadn't been so surprised by Jordan's macho attempt to use the male version of an *I'm-better-than-you* card when he introduced himself. If they hadn't just had the conversation about Jordan's ex, she would have thought his behavior signified jealousy. Now, she was suspicious, wondering if he was pretending for her benefit because he thought she was jealous of Stacy Blaut and wanted to return the favor.

A throat was cleared, and she heard Daniel mumble a quick introduction. "Sutton. Daniel Sutton."

The lights in her apartment went out. Kaylee heard the door close and the shuffle of footsteps moving toward her before Jordan, clearly unimpressed, came back with, "Nice. Well, I'm sure we'll see you around."

Having caught up to Kaylee, Jordan leaned down and pressed a quick kiss onto her lips before taking her hand in his to tug her in the opposite direction from her ex. He didn't bother to further acknowledge Daniel when they passed him on the sidewalk, but he did watch through narrowed lids over the top of Kaylee's head until he saw the taillights of Daniel's car disappearing around the corner. There was a fierce look in his eyes when he murmured quietly under his breath, "Thanks for stopping by—douche bag."

* * *

From the outside, Hawthorne Grove's public library looked completely disenchanting.

But for a dim glow emanating from the few solar powered lamps strategically placed to light the front walk and the stone steps to the entry, the building was quiet and dark; empty—as any public structure after hours should be. Inside, however, was another story. Lit by an energy only those possessed with a working knowledge of magic could detect, Hawthorne Grove's large public library's interior glowed softly with a warm incandescence, and the low hum of quiet male voices belied the vacant appearance of the building from the outside.

Chin high and shoulders straight, Esmerelda Seville made her way between a long corridor of books toward an alcove set into the stone wall at the end. A thick wooden door, banded with heavy wrought iron bands gone black over the passing of several hundred centuries, appeared in the center just as she drew up before it.

"*Aisimentum.*" She quickly whispered the old Latin word she had heard Alastair use previously when requesting liberty of passage and the heavy door swung inward, allowing her entry into a cavernous round room that appeared to be the central chamber of what was once an old abbey or cathedral. Circling the chamber was a chain of similar wood and iron-banded doors that lead one through lengthy corridors to various secret vaults and anterooms where she now knew the many precious volumes of Hawthorne Grove's magical history and lore—both the immediate, and that of ancient times—was kept.

Alastair Skurlock, one of the chosen and most recent Keepers of the Lore, was in one of those chambers—enchanted and be-spelled rooms that strong magic kept hidden from the day-to-day patrons of the library. She needed only to find the right one—but there were so many! She sighed. Why couldn't he simply have met her at the door, like a proper date?

Because Seville's weren't allowed to have proper dates, she reminded herself. But this wasn't a date, exactly. She needed something only Alastair could give her, and tonight was the only night she had—the only night she *would have* for a very long time—to throw caution to the wind and tempt the hands of Fate to get it. Carefully counting her footsteps as she went, Esmerelda managed to make it seventy two full paces and one half-step forward before a door opened to her left.

Alastair walked out, his brow pulled into a frown, and closed the door behind him. Had he sensed her presence? Of course he had. Breaching the sanctuary would have been a dead giveaway if he hadn't known she was here from the moment she stepped foot on Keeper's soil.

He spotted her almost immediately and hurried to her side, a ferocious looking scowl replacing the frown on his face. "Esmerelda? Dammit, you have to go back!" he growled. "You know you can't be in here."

She did know, but at the moment, she did not care. Nor did she particularly like the way he was glaring at her. "Serephina and Mortianna are gone. They flew out this morning to spend the weekend in New York City. I just thought you might like to know. I'll be alone."

Any minute now, she knew he would do what he must and signal the guards to take her away if they weren't already on high alert and headed her way. It was his job, his duty as Keeper of the Lore to maintain the sanctity of the sanctuary and she knew she only had a matter of seconds to say what she had come to say. But now that she was here, staring into those piercing gray eyes of his, she was suddenly quite uncertain of the sanity of her goal.

"Esmerelda—" His eyes closed for a second and when he opened them again, something feral flickered in his gaze. She heard a noise. The guards. They had been alerted and her time was running out. She could hear their footsteps, heading in her direction and picking up speed and she didn't stick around to see the rest of his reaction. Instead, she turned, sucked in a breath, took a step and started counting.

"Seventy-one, seventy, sixty-nine—" Before she reached the count of fifty, she was in a full-out run, headed back toward the door she'd come in through, trying to make it out before the guards arrived—and she could hear Alastair keeping time with her paces just three steps behind—in case she didn't quite make it.

Chapter Fifteen

Jordan was quiet for most of the ride back to his place. He couldn't stop thinking about how Kaylee had reacted when she'd opened her door and found her ex-fiance standing there with a smile on his face. That she had reacted at all was causing most of his problem. There was no way he could guess what had been going on in her thoughts at the time, either, but he could imagine none of it was pretty. Still, she'd gone silent for so long, crazy things had started going on in his head and for the first time in a long time, he'd felt panic.

He hadn't known what to expect. He'd seen her blanch when she realized who was at her door and he'd waited, watching the interactions between them in silence when what he'd really wanted to do was plant his fist right between the guy's eyes. He could clearly read lust on her ex-fiance's features, but he wasn't about to bow out like Mr. Nice Guy and give the scum a free pass to hurt Kaylee again. Anyone who would walk out on a woman like Kaylee the way he had done...

Glancing over at her now, Jordan almost winced. She had her head turned and was looking out the window at the scenery as it passed even though it was really too dark for her to see anything. She was still too quiet to suit him, though, and he wondered if her silence was a thoughtful kind of quiet, full of questions about life, maybe, over which she was currently musing? Or was it the more dangerous, forced kind—the sort that kicked into place by an inner fury so great the only way she could hold herself together after the shock of unexpectedly seeing Daniel again was to keep her silence; to hold her pain and fury inside?

Granted, those few words she had said to Daniel before he'd made his presence known had been spoken in a kind of cool, detached, dead-pan tone. Maybe he was over-reacting? Maybe she really didn't care that the man she had been in love with for years had just came back to town? Daniel had made it patently clear he would like to step back into her life, to resume the relationship they'd shared before he left town but Kaylee hadn't given any sort of sign that said she was interested.

But then, Daniel had touched her. He'd put his fingers in Kaylee's hair, and that was when Jordan thought he was going to lose it. Just barely, he'd managed to hold his own rising anger in check long enough to usher Kaylee past the man and out of her own apartment. True, he'd got a few digs in at the guy, but he'd done it for Kaylee, mostly. He only hoped she could tell he was trying to make her see without saying that her real friends knew her schedule, but her douchy ex, he didn't even know Kaylee didn't work weekends.

Or, hell, Jordan admitted to himself, maybe it was jealousy—straight up. All he knew for sure right now was that he saw red every time he thought of Daniel Sutton's hands anywhere near any part of Kaylee's body. He wasn't too keen on him having his eyes on her, either, but what he really needed to know was how Kaylee felt—about both of them.

She hadn't said more than two words since he'd closed the door on his Dodge after helping her inside back at her apartment, and those were just a quickly muttered, "Thank you." Had she been using the quiet time during their ride to figure out a way to tell him she wouldn't be seeing him again?

Jordan ran a hand over his face and forced himself to concentrate on the road. It wasn't easy, what with his thoughts racing around in his head like an over-anxious schoolgirl before her first date, chanting a single, vastly important question with every turn: How would Daniel Sutton's return to Hawthorne Grove affect his and Kaylee's budding relationship?

Surprisingly, not ten minutes later, when she slid out of the truck and followed him around to the side door to wait while he unlocked it so they could go inside, the first words out of Kaylee's mouth were an accusation. "You were *trying* to make him angry, weren't you? Those little digs about your wealth and fame—those were intentional, meant to make him feel inferior—or to make *you* feel superior."

"No, I *made* him angry," Jordan corrected, suddenly bristling at her tone. Flipping on the lights as he led her through the mudroom and kitchen to his living room, he continued, "There was no *try* to it, and yes, there is a difference. I did it on purpose, which was more than *you* did. I guess his showing up out of the blue like that had you rattled?"

Woof!

Sarge ran in from the other room to greet them and Jordan leaned down to give him a pat, glad for a little distraction ... and affection.

"I was paying attention. So you admit you made him mad on purpose—but why? Is that some kind of man thing? You wanted to feel superior, right? To feel like you were better than him? You were rude, Jordan."

Sarge nosed Kaylee's hand, looking up at her with big brown eyes that encouraged her to do some petting of her own, which she did, but only half-heartedly as her focus was still on the argument she was currently having with Jordan.

"Yes, well, *you* weren't. I figured one of us should be. The creep dumped you virtually on the eve of your wedding, then has the nerve to try and waltz back into your life like nothing happened? Four years, Kaylee! He's been out of your life for four years, and now—" Jordan squeezed his eyes closed for a second, then shrugged out of his coat. He tossed it, his keys, and the movies he'd rented for them to watch this weekend onto the coffee table. "Make yourself comfortable. I'll get food started."

She followed him back into the kitchen, Sarge trotting along behind her. "Again, I want to know why?"

Jordan shrugged and rubbed at his neck and growled low, from somewhere in the back of his throat. Why was this happening? Especially tonight? The last thing he wanted right now was to be fighting with her. "I was—feeling him out, I suppose, alright? Anger is not the same as jealousy, you know, and I wanted to see which one he displayed in relation to you."

Her head was cocked at that jaunty angle, tilted slightly to one side while she peered up at him, a thousand questions swimming in her beautiful eyes. "Because you want me to think you're jealous, right? Because of my reaction to the visit from your ex-girlfriend today?"

"No! No, Kaylee, it was because of my reaction to *your* visit, the one from your ex-*fiance*. You remember him, right? The man you were going to *marry*? The man you once *loved*? Big difference between your relationship with him and mine with Stacy Blaut, Kaylee, and regardless of what you choose to believe, I reacted exactly the way I did to your...your friend Daniel because I *am* jealous!" He stopped and turned to stare at her. "Don't you see? He was *there*, Kaylee. He was there, before me, and he—he had a big part of your life all to himself, while I—"

Biting back a string of curses, he stopped again,

then shook his head. "He hurt you, Kaylee. So bad you still can't enjoy the promise of a happily ever after in at least one romantic movie that I know of, and from the sound of things, he's looking for an easy way back into your life so he can do it all over again."

Jordan went to the fridge, scrambling around inside, looking for something, anything to pull out but came back empty-handed instead. She had him tangled up in knots and this whole thing with Daniel was making him say things without thinking them through. Everything suddenly felt chaotic and out of order and now she had a happy little glow in her eyes, the kind that was making his stomach do somersaults.

"You think he wants me back? And if he does, what makes you think he would hurt me again?"

His eyes narrowed. Was she insane? Only an idiot wouldn't... "I would! Want you back, I mean, not hurt you."

Slamming the refrigerator door shut with a quick kick, Jordan turned to try and explain. His reasons for trying to do so didn't make sense, even to him, but he needed her to understand. "Kaylee, love—*real* love—it isn't—it isn't like what I suspect your Daniel has in mind, at least not this time."

She frowned. "What do you mean?"

"I mean—it's not something you fall in and out of, you know? And when you're in it, you damn sure don't disappear for four years, then show up one day out of the blue hoping to pick up where you left off. If you're in it, you're in it for good.

When it's real, you never come out. You might wish you could turn it off once in a while when you're in pain, when you're hurting, but…"

"Says Dr. Romance himself," Kaylee scoffed. Pushing past him, she opened the refrigerator and pulled out a stalk of celery, which she promptly bit into. "You're speaking from experience, I suppose. Was it Stacy? Were you in love with her?"

"I thought I was, but as it turned out, it was more like I was in *convenience* with her, Kaylee. I needed someone and she was there. She was great at social functions, business dinner schmoozing, things like that. We lived together. I thought I loved her. It was easier for her to be nearby."

She stared at him, one eyebrow arched high in question. "Did you sleep with her?"

Jordan groaned. He knew he could lie and deny it, but what would that say about the kind of man he was? Still, he was afraid if he told her the truth she would walk away …

"Does it matter? You asked me if I loved her and the truth is *no*. I was *never* in love with Stacy Blaut and she was never in love with me."

* * *

Eyes narrowed, Kaylee propped on the back of one of his dining chairs, one hand on her hip, the other motioning pointedly toward him with the stalk of celery while Sarge sat on the floor beside her, his eyes ping-ponging between the two of them, stopping now and again to look hopefully at the celery. "How do you know?"

This was the question she'd been trying to get to, the only one that was really important—for him and for her. Did he know what love was? Was he sure he understood? Because after everything she had been through with Daniel, Kaylee didn't think she could handle uncertainty on his part. If he wasn't sure ...

She watched him carefully, ignoring the way her heart was fluttering in her chest while she waited, almost without breathing, to see how he would answer. He seemed so shook up. It was kind of cute, a little sexy, but at the same time, it was pretty terrifying. Was she really ready for this? There was no time to debate the question because he was already answering.

"I know because I *never* felt for her the things I feel for you, Kaylee Dean. Not. Even. Close."

There was real emotion in the husky sound of his words but it was the fierce, burning look in his eyes that took her breath away. She almost dropped her celery. "Jordan? Are you saying you love me?"

His eyes closed for a moment then popped open again. "I'm definitely saying I think your ex-fiance doesn't love you. Maybe he loves the idea of having you in his life again, but—he came back for *something*, Kaylee."

Kaylee couldn't deny she'd felt a little pinch of disappointment when he didn't immediately say yes, but then, this whole day had been filled with so many emotional ups and downs she also couldn't say she wasn't relieved to not have to deal with a full-on confession of his undying love. "And you think he came back for me—but you don't think I should take him?"

His expression became guarded. "Would you?"

There was such a wealth of carefully unspoken inquiry in his question Kaylee didn't have to wonder if the idea of her getting back with Daniel bothered him. It was a strange moment, one where her entire world seemed precariously balanced upon her answer while for Jordan, his question represented a ledge—one from which he was fully prepared to jump if he did not like what her answer revealed.

"Would you, Kaylee?"

Unable to bear the dread creeping into his gaze, she shook her head. "No."

Both his hands flew out, arms spread wide, and he stared at her, his jaw slack with amazement. "Then why are we even having this crazy conversation?"

Kaylee tilted her head and peered up at him, as if seriously considering his question. Finally, she grinned, letting him know he was off the hook for the moment. "Because you're sexy when you're all riled up like that?"

Jordan groaned and held out his hands, wiggling his fingers in an invitation to curl hers around them. "Teasing me, were you?"

The look in her eyes all promise, she shook her head and moved close to him, stopping only when she could no longer move forward. She reached up to twine her arms around his neck. "No, but I am about to."

Her chin tilted upward and she knew he had to have felt her breath catch as easily as she had heard his swiftly indrawn, but without breaking eye contact, he held his arms straight out from his body, refusing to touch her.

Kaylee frowned. "Jordan, what the heck do you think you are you doing?"

"A promise is a promise," he reminded her.

"Right." Kaylee struggled to keep the disappointment out of her voice. She tightened her arms around his neck. "So, if you're not going to ravish me, what are we going to do now that you've got me home with you, Jordan H. Parker—*Forbes* famous ex-CEO and billionaire?"

"Dinner? Movies?" He tilted his head. "Actually, I just had the perfect idea."

Her brow rose. "Oh?"

Jordan nodded. "A swim in the lake behind the house."

"Are you crazy? The water's probably freezing out there!"

He shrugged. "A shower then, preferably icy cold."

"I don't think I understand."

"Strings, Kaylee. I promised no strings, but every time you get near me, I'm the one who gets tied in knots."

"Hmm," she murmured, leaning into him before rising up on her tip-toes to kiss his chin. "You know, that's why I started a pet grooming business."

Sarge must have heard the word *pet* because he came trotting over and nosed first Kaylee then Jordan before trying to wriggle his way between them.

Jordan frowned. "Ah, unfortunately I am not a dog, in case that slipped your notice."

Kaylee chuckled. "No, you are definitely not a dog, but maybe there's a little bit of animal in you? My clients tell me I'm pretty darn handy at unraveling things."

Chapter Sixteen

The bell over the shop's door jingled melodically, signaling the arrival of what she thought was today's 214 but Esmerelda Seville was neither available for nor prepared to greet her customer.

"Quilt, quilt, where is the dang quilt?" she muttered while digging through every nook and cranny, both material and magical, of Seville's Antiquities and Collectibles for the black-and-white checkered coverlet Serephina had set aside in anticipation of this very moment. Her hair was completely disheveled, her clothes looked slept in —which wasn't true at all—she'd left them pooled on the floor beside the bed exactly where they had fallen last night, and her focus was off. But she *was* here, and she was determined to deliver the quilt she'd arguably skipped a trip to NYC to deliver... only she could not find the thing.

Riffling quickly through the only chest she hadn't yet searched, she growled her annoyance to the mostly empty shop, mumbling, "Serephina is going to kill me! Where is the blasted quilt?"

"Maybe if you had been *home* last night instead of slipping off to consort with the enemy, you'd have gotten my text telling you I put the quilt in your room."

Serephina's voice was as cold as chipped ice, and Esmerelda would bet her eyes reflected more of the same. She froze, lifted her hands from the chest, closed it, and then stood, slowly wiping her hands together as she turned to face her sisters with what she hoped was a calm expression. Ignoring both the not-so-veiled reference to Serephina's guess about where she'd been last night and the cutting look of accusation in her sister's gaze, Esmerelda forced her breathing to resume, encouraged her suddenly heightened heart rate to slow to a more normal rhythm, and casually propped her hands on her hips. Offering up a wide smile of welcome, she said, "Well! You two are home early."

Taking a chance the simple greeting would be enough, she started forward toward the front of the shop and the stairs. If the quilt was in her room, she needed to get back there and get it before the lady who was coming here to pick it up arrived. All she had to do was get past her sisters.

She'd taken maybe three steps before a thick, soft bundle of sweetly fragrant cloth hit her in the face, blocking her vision and her path. On the other side of it, Mortianna's words were as forceful as the hand she was using to shove the previously missing quilt into Esmerelda's hands.

"Go on without me. I'll take care of everything. It'll be fine! You've got nothing to worry about! Well, Merry, maybe you'd like to explain how Jordan and Kaylee managed to *miss* their flight? Or, you could tell us how you reacted when you discovered Stacy Blaut was no longer *in* New York, but visiting her old buddy Jordan Parker here in good old Hawthorne Grove? I would love to hear that!"

Reaching up with both hands, Esmerelda pulled the checkered fabric out of Mortianna's grasp to cradle it carefully in her own arms, trying to ignore both her sisters' furious gazes and the way her fingers were shaking while she smoothed them over the delicate cloth. *Miss Blaut was in Hawthorne Grove?*

"Or, just for fun," Mortianna added, continuing with a narrow-eyed glare, "why don't you give us the full story, recounting everything that happened when, after four years of absence, Daniel Sutton suddenly showed up at Kaylee Dean's front door?"

Esmerelda could literally feel her skin losing color and she opened her mouth to ask when all of this had happened—she would carefully ignore the question of how her sisters *knew* it had—but, apparently, Mortianna wasn't finished.

"It must be quite an amusing tale, the story of how both our charges ex's managed to arrive in Hawthorne Grove both without our knowing and on the *one* day when Feeny and I just happened to be out of town, magically stranded because we were hundreds of non-magical miles away!"

Esmerelda's mouth worked, but no words came out. If everything her sister had said were true, they could be in big trouble with the CHG. Worse, it was all her fault, and she knew it.

Guilt, the same strain which had been simmering inside her over her hastily made choice since yesterday, slowly heated to a mortifying boil, but Mortianna didn't seem to care.

"Twenty *seven* years, Esmerelda! Twenty seven *years*! We've managed to get through two point seven decades without making mistakes like this, and now—how *could* you?"

The tearful accusation in her sister's eyes and voice heaped more guilt onto the fire of embarrassment and remorse already burning inside her, until...

How could *she*?

Esmerelda's back went stiff with indignation. For the past twenty seven years—since the day all three of them had agreed to a binding contract with the CHG—*Mortianna* had done her level best to screw up everything Serephina and herself tried to do to honor it. And now *she* was pointing fingers? Her chin came up and she leveled a narrow-eyed glare on her sibling. One brow arched high—almost as high as the anger that had suddenly blown up to replace the guilt she'd been feeling over the possibly disastrous repercussions her choice had created—and opened her mouth again to remind Mortianna of just how many mistakes she and Serephina had fielded for *her* when Mortianna sighed, gave an almost piteous shake of her head, and asked, "How could you do this, Merry?"

It was something in her tone that clued Esmerelda in.

Locking gazes with Mortianna, she finally caught the tiny spark of warning almost hidden in her eyes that seemed to scream *keep-your-mouth-shut-and-follow-my-lead*. Relief mingled with suspicion over whatever Mortianna was attempting to do and she became suddenly wary. This was just the sort of situation she generally tried to avoid. Should she keep silent and let whatever little game Mortianna was playing with Serephina play itself out? Or should she just step up and take responsibility for her actions, admit she'd wanted them to go to NYC and leave her behind? That she'd ignored her responsibilities to Mr. Parker and Miss Dean to slip away and enjoy at least one night of ...

No, no, no she could practically hear Mortianna screaming in her head. Admit nothing and deny everything was Morty's motto and was more often than not her go-to piece of advice. But Esmerelda was back to feeling guilty over what she'd done—although she still wasn't exactly clear on just how much that entailed—and she wasn't sure she could make herself keep quiet in such a potentially wired for destruction situation like this.

"Mortianna, I—"

"Should concentrate, Merry," Serephina all but ordered. "We've a customer at the door. We can discuss this later, and yes, we will discuss what you've done. For now, however, let's get that glamour up and greet the lady of the morning with a smile."

Relieved to put off the inevitable, if only for a few minutes more, Esmerelda turned and fled the storeroom, determined to at least get the delivery of the quilt right. It may not be much, but it was one less mistake to be laid at her door if they had to face the CHG.

* * *

Kaylee woke to a stream of warm, pale blue light spilling across her face from the window of one of Jordan's spare bedrooms. Stretching, she swiped her hands across the covers and her palm brushed something hard. The snow globe. She didn't know why, but she'd tucked it into her coat pocket last night before she'd slipped past Daniel and out of her apartment to wait for Jordan outside.

The thing had become a talisman for her—a good luck charm of sorts that kept bad things at bay—and she just seemed to feel better whenever she was holding it in her palm, like now. Shaking the fragile glass ball carefully, she held it up into the beam of sunlight and peered inside, watching the snow swirl and fall in mindless, untraceable patterns, filling the empty spaces between the trees and the grounds surrounding the beautiful old Victorian house inside while her thoughts played over the cheesily romantic evening she had spent with Jordan.

A few kisses after their conversation about

Daniel, Kaylee had helped Jordan put together one of the best baked nacho dishes she'd ever tasted. Jordan had started a fire, and they'd curled up on the sofa in front of the television and watched two of the three movies back to back before he'd asked the question of the evening: did she want to go home, or would she stay the night with him?

Her first excuse was the one of no clothes, which Jordan had gotten around by offering one of his old t-shirts for her to sleep in. Kaylee reached down to pull the material close to her nose for another sniff—it smelled clean, of course, but there was still some lingering remnant of his scent within the fabric. It was dreamy. She'd had a hard time falling asleep last night for thinking about it, about him, and about how easy it would be to push back the covers and join him across the hall. All she had to do was say the word, and she could be in his bed—but she wasn't sure she was ready to take that final step.

Like the glass surrounding the house inside the snow globe, her relationship with Jordan was much too fragile at the moment. At least she thought it was. It needed time to grow a little, to mature, to strengthen before they introduced sex into the equation. Especially now that Daniel was back in Hawthorne Grove.

Kaylee rolled over, letting the snow globe slip out of her hands and onto the counterpane as easily as her thoughts slid into a whirlpool of what-ifs concerning her relationships past and present. Why had Daniel come back, really? She wondered if what Jordan had suggested was true—that he'd come back for her—and the thought that it might be made her angry. Did Daniel really think she would have sat around pining for his return for the past four years?

Isn't that exactly what you did do? Her conscience snipped, and she scoffed at its brutal honesty. It was true, she had waited. But then, she'd pulled herself together and gotten a life, albeit an empty one. And then, Jordan had arrived and changed everything. He'd gotten her out again—out of her apartment and out of her head. Out of the shell she had built around herself to protect her heart.

For one uncomfortable minute, she tried to imagine her life without Jordan's presence in it, and was surprised to realize just how empty it would seem. Had she really had such a gaping void in her world? How was it possible she hadn't known? A quick knock sounded about a half-second before the doorknob turned and Jordan came in bearing a tray laden with breakfast goodies that were still steaming, Sarge loping happily in by his side.

"Good morning, sleeping beauty. I hope you're hungry. I made a little of everything I had. Blueberry waffles, buttered strawberry muffins, bacon, eggs scrambled or fried, and even a helping of grits and some hash browns."

Kaylee slid back against the pillows, feeling only slightly self conscious because she was half naked beneath the covers he was even now sliding the tray over on. It caught on a seam and he reached over her to tug at the quilt, giving it a quick flick before she could think to warn him. "Oh, wait!"

But her cry came too late. The snow globe rolled over the edge of the bed and landed with a watery crash on the hardwood floor not two inches from the cushioned throw rug that might have saved it.

"What the heck? Where did that come from?" he asked, but now oblivious to her borrowed nightwear and bare thighs, she was out of bed in a flash, standing with both hands over her mouth, her eyes burning with unreasonable tears as she stared down at a watery pool speckled with bits of white foam surrounding a house turned on it's side and two tiny, fake trees.

Vision blurred, her gaze swept up to meet Jordan's while her mind replayed a memory of the day they'd met outside the antique shop and she recalled how every time she'd looked into the globe afterward she'd thought only of him. Looking back down at the house now lying oddly on its side in the shallow puddle at her feet, she thought it odd that the lights seemed to have had gone off and the house now looked empty and cold inside.

Her eyes widened and snapped up as she cast a quick, anxious glance at Jordan, suddenly terrified the globe's destruction was some sort of terrible omen, warning her of bad things to come. Pushing the thought from her mind, she started forward to clean up the mess, but Jordan's hand shot out, holding her back.

"Kaylee, stop. There's glass everywhere and you're bare-footed. Don't move. Or, better yet, get back into bed while I go get a broom or something."

Sarge nudged her, edging her toward the bed and she nodded, but he didn't quite leave fast enough. The tears blurring her vision and scalding her eyes which had shown up for reasons she didn't understand decided to multiply much too rapidly for her to hold them back. A sob wrenched itself from her throat, and Jordan stopped, his hand on the doorknob, to look back at her.

"Kaylee, are you okay?"

Once again, she shook her head, forcing her hands to move away from her mouth where they had hovered in horror until now, and pushed them down to her sides. "Yes, I'm fine. I—It's just a snow globe. It wasn't even special to me. I mean, I only bought it a few weeks ago, and so I haven't had it that long, really, and ... I don't even know why I'm crying!"

A frown drew his brows downward. "Is that the one you picked up at Seville's the day we met?"

She couldn't trust herself to speak with the rush of tears now clogging her throat and making her nose want to run, so she just nodded her head again. Within seconds, he was back across the room, cuddling her close to his chest and all she could think of was how warm he felt while everything else around her seemed to have gone cold. He tilted her chin up with his thumb.

"I'm sorry, Kaylee."

He leaned down, following his almost gruffly spoken words with a soft kiss of apology that, for reasons she had neither time nor inclination to try and understand, quickly turned into more.

Chapter Seventeen

Jordan had been battling his crazy desire for Kaylee all morning, since way before he walked into his spare bedroom carrying a spur-of-the-moment breakfast tray and saw her lying there in a stream of early morning sunlight, looking all sleep-soft and sexy in his old t-shirt.

He'd thought about her all night as he lay sleepless and aroused in his lonely bed, recalling just how close she actually was and how few steps he'd need to take to join her in the room next to his, but through sheer force of will, he had managed to keep his "no strings" promise and his distance.

But when she leaned into his body, her face tilted eagerly into his kiss and her fingers twisted themselves deep into the thick strands of his hair, tugging his head down to hers for a much more thorough exploration of his lips and mouth, an all male primal instinct kicked in and he forgot all about the "no strings" promise he had made.

His groan came up from somewhere in his chest,

spilling into the suddenly electrified air around them in the form of a low growl, and it was all he could do to keep his movements slow and controlled as he pulled her closer, fitting her tighter against his body while his mouth feasted hungrily upon hers.

In a gentle sweep, he pulled his palms down the length of her back to the sloping curve at the top of her hips. He would have stopped there—at least, that's what he told himself—if he hadn't felt the slight forward tilt of her lower body toward his, arching ever nearer the part of him that ached to be with her so badly the simple action dragged another deep-chested growl from his lips.

Breaking away from her kiss was torture, but his mouth was determined to taste more of her: the shadowy curve of creamy skin just beneath her jaw, the tempting, slender column of her throat, the delicate flesh of her dainty little earlobe, which he sucked between his lips for a quick nibble.

Her gasp in reaction did crazy things to him, making him frenzied with need and he took two steps forward, pushing her toward the bed until her calves came up against the mattress and she could go no further. Taking both her hands in his, he turned with her so that he was against the bed and would have pulled her down with him onto it if he hadn't caught a glimpse of the breakfast tray still sitting on the bed from the corner of his eye.

Squeezing his eyes tight in an attempt to will the image of the tray blocking their path to the bed away, he slid his arms around her again and tightened his fists into the material of his shirt at her waist. His lips nuzzled her neck until he found her earlobe again and he nibbled once, twice, and yet again before whispering, "Kaylee? Sweetheart, we have two choices. One, we stop before one or both of us tumbles into your breakfast or the shards of glass still lying on the floor, or I pick you up and carry you to my room where we will *not* stop until I have you completely naked and writhing beneath me in my bed."

Lifting his head again, he leaned back and opened his eyes to find hers staring, passion-warmed and limpid, into his and he cursed himself silently for not simply picking her up and taking her to his bed to have his way with her. But somehow he knew the choice of whether or not they made love this morning needed to be hers.

He felt her grip loosen and then slide from his scalp down across his shoulders to rest against his chest. The passion he'd seen a moment before in her eyes cooled, even as she smoothed her fingers across the taut muscles beneath her hands. Her tone almost regretful, she said, "I want you. More than I've ever wanted anything or anyone, I think."

Jordan didn't have to ask. He could hear the hesitation in her tone. But he did anyway. "But?"

Her lips twisted ruefully and she pushed slightly away from him. "But, I think we should wait."

Something pinched sharply in his gut—a feeling he recognized as a swift kick of regret—and he winced, even though he tilted his head in accepting acknowledgment of her decision. Then, he straightened, forcing away his disappointment, and after twining their fingers together again, he arched a brow in question. "Just for clarity's sake, do you mean we should wait, like, until after breakfast, or ... ?"

"We should wait until ... until further notice, Jordan Parker," Kaylee told him, her brow furrowed into a mock scowl which cleared immediately when she could no longer hold back her laughter at his teasing tone. His immediate and overly dramatic sigh of disappointment caused another quick burst of laughter to spill from her lips, which he caught with his own, but this time he managed to keep his hands still and steady and his kiss light and undemanding.

Half an hour later, after he had cleared away the broken glass and other pieces from the snow globe and she had appeased her grumbling stomach with at least half of the yummy breakfast he'd brought to her upstairs, Kaylee hurried through Jordan's bedroom into the large, luxurious bathroom on the other side for a quick shower, her lips still tingling with pleasure from his kisses.

The warm spray of water sluiced over her, reminding her with sultry images in clear, vivid detail just how hot she had burned beneath the heat of Jordan's touch. She hadn't meant to kiss him—not like she had, anyway. And she hadn't meant to crave the feel of his hands on her body, her fingers on his skin, but she had—oh, so much. There was no way she could honestly deny how badly she had wanted to give in: to him, to her desire to be with him, but when she'd looked into his eyes and realized he'd never actually said he loved her—that had made her hesitate and set off great big warning bells around her heart that pealed with the demand to proceed with calm and deliberate caution.

Shutting off the shower, she grabbed a towel for her hair and wrapped another one around her middle before padding across the bedroom once again to call for Jordan through the door. "I'm out now. Won't take but a minute to dry and dress, so you can go ahead and start the truck if you want."

He'd left some of his old clothes on the foot of his bed for her since she'd left her apartment without her own and she hurried to slip into them now in case he decided he needed to open the bedroom door so she could *clarify* what he thought she'd said.

Remembering how smoothly he'd turned what could have been a far too serious moment into one laced with humor and fun, her lips curled upward into a smile before she shook her head. With Jordan, the one thing she knew she could count on was his penchant for random moments of spontaneous humor—like when he pretended to have conversations with Sarge. His humor was just one of the many things she'd come to love about him. She only hoped her decision to stay out of his bed for now hadn't ruined her chances for discovering more.

* * *

"What in the world are you wearing?" Jo asked the moment she slid into a seat beside her at Sam's. Her eyes did a quick skim of the thick charcoal gray turtleneck sweater and heather gray sweatpants she wore—both of which were obviously too big for her—and widened. "Forget I asked ... is he as good in bed as he looks like he should be?"

Kaylee sipped at her coffee, ignoring the blush suddenly heating her cheeks, and batted a hand at her sister in admonition.

"What?" Jo demanded. "You're wearing his *clothes* already. It's just a matter of time before you'll be wearing his ring, too, if my intuition is on —and it usually is, Kaylee. Don't even try to deny it. But I'm guessing there's at least one more thing of his that doesn't belong in his closet or on your finger that you've tried on for size sometime within the past twenty-four hours. Am I right or am I right?"

If she had allowed her blush at the thoughts her sister's comments brought to mind to answer for her, Kaylee could have gotten away without admitting she still hadn't slept with Jordan, but her conscience wouldn't let her.

"No, you aren't, and do call Guinness because, for once, the great Jo Dean Leavy's notorious sixth sense has failed her. You lose, Sis. This time you missed your guess. But you're not too terribly far from the mark," Kaylee's ridiculously brutal conscience forced her to add. "Have you been here long?"

"Long enough to be forced to sit through reacquainting myself with Daniel Sutton. He was here when I came in and he saw me before I could duck back out the door. Apparently, his love dumped him, but not before he realized how terribly he had treated you when he left. He says he came back to make amends."

Kaylee looked at her hands. "Jordan said pretty much the same thing."

"He mentioned he ran into you and some guy at your apartment last night. I told him it was your husband. Also might have mentioned Jordan has a shotgun and enough money to pay off anyone who might hear the sound of it going off if he dared get close to you."

Kaylee's eyes flew wide and she stared at her sister in panic. "Jo! You didn't! Don't you know that could be construed as—"

Jo rolled her eyes and waved a hand to indicate that she could calm down before she popped a vein or something, as she was fond of saying. "Of course I know, and of course I didn't. But that doesn't mean I didn't want to. The guy is pure scum and you know it."

"You never told me that four years ago." It was the truth and they both knew it. Before Daniel had walked out of her life, everyone in Kaylee's family and circle of friends had thought him the cat's meow. Or, that was what they told her, anyway.

"That was before he broke your heart and crushed your spirit. I never want to see that happen to you again, Kaylee. I won't *let* it happen. But I don't think I have anything to worry about. Not anymore," she said, her gaze flicking toward Jordan an instant before she cocked her head in his direction. "Did he tell you he loves you?"

Kaylee let her gaze linger on him longer than she should have. He glanced up at her and tilted his head up in acknowledgment of her stare. Looking quickly away, she shook her head.

"Ah, that explains why you're here so early this morning and not still curled up with him in his bed. You told him you love him, though, right?"

Kaylee plunked her cup down hard on the table and narrowed her eyes. "Did I ask this many nosy, personal questions when you were dating Michael?"

Jo shook her head no. "You asked *more*, Kaylee Dean, and I'm not letting you off the hook without an answer. Not that I need it after your attempt to sidestep the question. You didn't tell him, did you?"

"No," Kaylee blurted. "I didn't, Jo, and I'm not sure I am going to. Not yet, anyway. I really don't want to rush things. Not this time."

"Rush?" Jo snorted. "Kaylee, dear, when it comes to relationships, you're the bloody, ever-lovin' tortoise, not the finish line dragging, to the point and back again before you can catch your breath hare."

"Yes, well, apparently I'm not slow enough. You saw how things turned out last time. If I had waited a few weeks more—" What? She wondered. Would she have refused Daniel's proposal? Would she have discovered his affections had moved on in time to save herself the pain and embarrassment of a broken engagement?

"Hey, don't look like that, Kaylee-bean." Jo's hand slid over to cover her own and gave it a little squeeze. "I love you and you know it. Maybe I'm being a little pushy where Jordan is concerned but you're my little sister and it's been a long time since I saw you this happy. I'd hate for you to let this new happiness I see slip away because you're too afraid to take that leap again, you know?"

Kaylee did know. She'd worried about the exact same thing less than an hour ago in Jordan's shower. But if she were going to mess things up between herself and Jordan, wasn't now the perfect time to do it—before her entire world became involved, the way it had with Daniel? She had a feeling she'd left things too late for that already but she couldn't bring herself to admit as much to her sister.

"I know you care, Jo, but I really need to take this slowly. If Jordan and I are meant to be, we will, but it has to happen when we are ready—not you, or Daniel, or anyone else who thinks we need to jump in with both feet before the spark disappears. If it's real, it won't. You know this. Look at you and Michael."

Jo smiled. "Oh, lord, don't you dare look at us! We've had more ups and downs in our lives than a roller coaster!"

"Yes," Kaylee agreed, and her brow arched high

as she continued. "But even you have to admit, for all the gut-wrenching twists and breathtaking turns your relationship with Michael has taken, it has been one hell of a ride. Now, tell me, am I right?"

Chapter Eighteen

Kaylee slid the cat's adoption papers into a folder and swept up both the packet and her purse before turning to Marc to explain why she needed to leave the shelter early today. "They're letter boxes—you know, where people used to keep their invitations and calling cards and such? Anyway, he buys them and restores them, but other than making them part of the visual aspect of his home décor, he says he hasn't any real use for them."

"So why doesn't he re-sell them? You said he restores them to their former glory, right? I thought those things were worth a lot of money."

Slipping her arms into her coat sleeves, Kaylee nodded. "Yes, but he doesn't want to sell them, Marc. He loves them. During the restoration process, he puts a part of himself into them, making each one even more special and unique than before."

"Oh, damn, girl you've got it bad. Puts a part of himself in? Special? Unique? It's just a matter of cleaning up the old and refurbishing it with a couple pieces of new, Kaylee. Jeez, you'd think Parker's some kind of old wood hero, to hear you tell it."

She glared at him. "Shut up, Marc. And you know what I meant. He just doesn't want to sell them. But neither does he want to keep them on display if he can't find a use for them, so—I'm going to help him with that."

Marc snickered. "Let me guess. You're going to the party shop to buy a thousand invitations? Gonna hand-address and special seal each one with a lipstick kiss before you pop them in his box?"

"No, you idiot. Well, not exactly, but something like that. I'll show you when I get one of them done, but there's Min," she said, having caught a glimpse of her cousin's yellow VW out the corner of her eye, "so I gotta go. Here are the Harvey's papers. Mrs. Harvey is supposed to be here in fifteen minutes. Thanks for taking care of it for me, hey?"

"Yeah, yeah, go on. Get out of here. Go buy your man some stationery," Marc said, waving her out the door. But it wasn't Mindy who caught her arm as soon as she stepped outside.

"Hey, whoa! I knew you'd come out of there eventually," Daniel said, steadying her after his unexpected presence caused her to lose her balance and then windmill her arms, flailing about to regain sure footing.

"Daniel, oh my—you almost made me bite the pavement!" One hand went to her chest while the other pushed down her coat. "Don't ever do that to me again!"

He had the decency to look contrite. Stuffing his hands into the back pocket of his jeans, he started walking with her toward the parking lot. "I'm sorry, but I didn't want you to leave before we had a chance to talk. Last time, you were—"

"On my way out," she finished for him. "And I'm kind of busy today, too. I have some errands to run. Shopping to do."

"That's fine. I can drive you," he offered.

"Can't, but thanks for the offer. Mindy's waiting for me." She lifted her hand and waved to her cousin, hoping Min would take it for the distress signal she almost felt it was, but Min only lowered her window enough to put a hand out and wave back.

Kaylee started toward the bright yellow car, but Daniel's hand caught her by the elbow, halting her. Keeping her expression carefully blank, she turned to stare at him. "Can't this wait, Daniel? I really don't think there is anything left for us to discuss. We were engaged, you met someone you loved more, and you left. End of story."

"Really, Kaylee? Can you honestly stand there and tell me that's all there was? You didn't miss me? Didn't think of me? That's not the Kaylee I know talking. Come on, darlin', this is *me*, Daniel, remember? And I—" He lifted a hand to her cheek, curving his palm around her jaw and it was all Kaylee could do to hold back her shudder. "I never stopped thinking about you, Kaylee. About the beautiful way you used to smile when I came up the graveled walk to your parent's house, and how you used to run out and meet me with a kiss."

He smiled at her, the same kind of smile he used to give her when she would run out to meet him, but Kaylee felt no regrets—only a fleeting sort of sadness—for him. When he'd left her, he had destroyed any warmth she might have felt for him and it wasn't coming back.

"I missed that," he continued. "I missed it, Kaylee, the same as I missed a thousand other things, beautiful, wonderful things about you. But mostly, every time I thought of you, I couldn't erase the memory of the haunted look of betrayal in your eyes the day I said goodbye."

Kaylee didn't look away from him but neither did she acknowledge his words. His gaze faltered, dropped away, and she thought for a minute he might give up and walk away, but then his eyes came swinging back to hers.

"I hurt you, Kaylee. I hurt you in a way that no woman deserves, and no matter how I tried, I could never quite get past that."

Oh, damn. Why had her parents ingrained good manners into her during her upbringing? Now she was going to have to say something. It was the least she could do. This was the first humanly decent thing he'd said to her since the day before he'd walked out of her life. "So you came back to apologize? Fine. Consider it said. You can go back now, to wherever you were staying before. We went our separate ways a long time ago, Daniel. We each have separate lives. You go back to yours and

I'll get on with mine."

"It's that guy, isn't it? The rich dude from *Forbes*?" He accused, a mulish, spurned look on his face. It smacked with a hint of assumed unfairness, and Kaylee almost laughed, so she bit her tongue.

"Jo told me you'd married the guy, but I didn't believe her. If you were married, you wouldn't have been going out for the weekend." *And I wouldn't be standing here talking to you*, Kaylee thought and then cocked her head to the side, considering. "But Jo and Michael go out all the time, and they're married. Or is it that you never planned to continue with the special evenings after you married that has you thinking no one else does?"

The look he gave her was imploring. "You're putting words in my mouth that I'm not saying, Kaylee. You never used to do that when we were engaged."

"Things change, Daniel."

"Yes, but they don't have to change in a bad way. That's why I came back, why I'm here today. Just—please. We need to talk, Kaylee. Privately, without you being in a rush to hurry off somewhere and without people trying to eavesdrop on our conversations," he said, motioning with his head over her shoulder where Kaylee could see Marc standing with one foot in the door of the entrance to the animal shelter, holding it open while glaring at Daniel over the top of her head.

Biting back a growl of frustration, Kaylee

glanced toward Mindy, then over her shoulder at Marc, desperately hoping for rescue from this conversation—one she certainly did not want to be having, especially not today—but finding none, she turned her gaze back to Daniel.

He hadn't really changed much in the past four years, she noticed. At least not physically. Sure there were a few new lines on his forehead and a few near his eyes, but ... there was something different in his eyes. Maybe he was telling the truth? Maybe he sincerely did regret how he'd left things with her, she rationalized, trying without success to justify an agreement to meet with him to talk. It wasn't like she owed him anything, that was for sure, but at the same time, she realized it wouldn't kill her to sit down for a minute or two and listen to what he had to say—for closure, if nothing else.

Ignoring the little flutter of panic she felt in her gut when she thought about what Jordan's reaction would be when he discovered what she was about to agree to do, she took a deep breath and said, "Alright, fine. We'll talk. But it'll have to be tomorrow and I can only promise a half an hour. We'll do coffee. At Sam—uh, Huntingdon's. Three thirty okay?"

Daniel smiled. "It's perfect. Thanks, Kaylee. I'll be waiting."

Unfortunately, Kaylee mumbled to herself as she walked away, feeling his eyes boring into her back the entire time.

She wound up spending every minute of her

shopping trip distracted, unsuccessfully trying to think of some way that didn't involve either Jordan, her sister, or her friends, to get out of meeting him there.

* * *

"No, no peeking! No peeking!" Kaylee squealed later that evening, smacking at Jordan's hands which were wont to wander as she led him from the living room while Sarge barked and ran excitedly back and forth to and from his kitchen, where the surprise she had prepared for Jordan waited on the hardwood table. "Okay, you can open your eyes."

Three rows of six boxes had been lined up, awaiting his inspection. She could hardly stand still while he opened the first one and said, "Ah, there are my keys."

"Yes! You didn't really lose them. I hope you're not mad, but I asked Sam to lift them for me—for this. But he knew I was going to give them back to you. Anyway, here's the garage door opener, and a mini-flashlight..."

He waited patiently while she went through each item she'd placed in the box, but his thoughts were on being stranded at Sam's all afternoon. Now he knew why. Kaylee had decided to surprise him and she needed the keys to his house to do it.

"This is now your 'going out of the house' box. You can put it there," she said, pointing toward the back entrance, "on that table by the door and you'll never have to wonder or remember where your things are because they each now have a definite place to be!"

Jordan stared at her, still feeling a bit quizzical, while her gaze switched back and forth between him and the letter boxes, a happy smile wreathing her lips the entire time. She was practically thrumming with a kind of child-like excitement and her particular brand of peppy zeal was catching. Jordan felt his own mood lighten, and he stepped forward. Eager to play whatever game she'd set out for them to play, he reached toward the second box in the first row. "And this one?"

His simple question set her off on an animated chorus of explanations as she carefully defined the purpose—purposes she personally had created, for each of the antique letter boxes in his meticulously chosen collection.

"...and this one," she said, pointing at the one Stacy had given him during her brief visit a few days ago as a sort of apology for her past behavior, "is for all the little things you're getting rid of, things you no longer want but haven't yet found the proper place or time to dispose of."

There was a little flash of something very akin to jealousy in her eyes when she looked at that box. Remembering what she'd said at her house the night of Stacy's unexpected visit about having to care an awful lot about him to be jealous, he grinned.

"We can 'get rid of' that particular box if you want, Kaylee," he offered, and he meant it. If

Stacy's gift made her uncomfortable he didn't want it there. But she was already shaking her head no.

"Not a chance and don't you dare. There is a definite time and place for endings, Jordan, and now, this box represents the place for yours. I thought it was perfect."

"I wholeheartedly agree," Jordan said, but he studied her intently, wondering what had motivated her to find a use for the letter boxes. "Was there a reason behind your sudden organizational spree? Other than helping me sort my haphazard and misguided life?"

A soft blush colored her cheeks and she looked away, her shoulders rising in a quick shrug. Was she embarrassed? She was, he decided, but he didn't understand why. "You love these boxes, Jordan. I can hear how much every time you mention one of them. But you said they were useless, taking up space, and you were going to get rid of them. I couldn't let you do that."

He felt the significance of what she had said in a place slightly north of his gut. Now he understood her almost shy hesitation a moment ago, the reason for her blushes and embarrassment. Her gift was revealing, personal, and she knew it. Doing what she'd done showed him, without a doubt, that she was the type of person who paid attention. Real attention. The kind that allowed her to see things one didn't even realize they were showing; to hear things he hadn't realized he'd said.

Pulling her close, he dropped a kiss on her forehead—she'd rested it against his chest in an attempt to avoid looking into his eyes, he guessed, but he wouldn't let her hide. Thumbing her chin upward, he said, "Thank you, Kaylee. And I mean that in a much deeper, far more sincere tone than it sounds. You're right—I do love them, even if I don't understand why. It's like, through the process of restoration, each one of them became a part of me somehow. But," he asked, pulling her into his arms again for a series of quick and yet ever-lingering kisses, "where are the chests for new beginnings? For the very rare and precious things that are starting right here and right now? The ones that will last an entire lifetime? An eternity?"

She was going to cry, he realized, when her eyelids fluttered quickly down to hide the swell of tears pooling in her eyes. But less than a heartbeat later, Jordan found that even he felt a suspicious sting beneath his eyelids when, eyes suddenly misty and soft, Kaylee pointed in the direction of his heart before patting her hand against her own and said, "Right in here."

Chapter Nineteen

I'll pick you up at the shelter on my way in, the the text said. *I. Have. Surprise.*

Kaylee switched off the engine and reached over to pick up her purse from the passenger seat but she didn't get out of the vehicle. She couldn't. Not yet. Jordan had a surprise for her? Last night he'd mentioned picking her up for lunch on his way back from Center, but he hadn't said anything about a surprise. Of course that may have been because she'd told him she couldn't do lunch because of her promise to meet Daniel at Huntingdon's, but ... darn it, what was the surprise? Swiping her thumb across the screen of her cell, she texted back: *What is it?*

She knew Daniel was waiting for her inside the coffee shop, and she was already ten minutes late, but she couldn't seem to make herself not wait for Jordan's answer. When it came, it was exactly what she expected it to be: *Not telling. You'll have to wait and see.*

"Grrrr!" she grumbled at his reply, but she was

smiling. Jordan had a surprise for her! Curious as a child at Christmas about what he might have picked up for her, she pushed open the door of her black SUV and stepped out. Slipping the strap of her purse over her head, she closed the door and locked it, then hit the touch screen on her phone again and typed: *I can hardly wait, but I suppose I must! Can I have a hint?*

His 'hint' was cryptic: *It's ... different.*

Different?

She waited for more, but no other words appeared on her screen so she tucked the phone into her back pocket and started for the coffee shop with an extra bit of spring in her step, her mood now in total contrast to the dread she had been feeling earlier about this meeting with Daniel. She managed a total of three steps before she thought about Jordan's text again and felt a grin tug at her lips. For some reason, she suddenly wanted to bounce into the store on her tiptoes, hopping like a kangaroo with the phrase *Jordan has a surprise!* sing-songing repeatedly from her lips, but she managed to temper her excitement and childlike glee—somehow.

Pushing open the door in the most adult-like manner she could muster at the moment, Kaylee bit down on her smile and waved to Sam, but it sprang right back into place when she turned around to scan the shop for Daniel. He was sitting in a booth near the window facing the parking lot, so he had to have seen her come in, but he hadn't made a move to greet her other than to tip his head back in acknowledgment when their gazes met.

With an internal groan, she made her way over to the booth. "Sorry I'm late. One of the other volunteers at the shelter had an appointment he couldn't miss and I couldn't get away until about ten minutes ago."

Daniel stood up right when she was about to sit down, which put their bodies in far too close a proximity for her comfort. She stepped back, but he slid his arm around her waist to steady her, pulling her closer just like he would have done four years ago...before he'd left her for another woman and almost ruined her life. It felt wrong.

All the happy excitement she'd felt only moments before fizzled away, leaving behind an unsettling kind of queasy feeling deep down in her stomach. Her smile disappeared and was immediately replaced with a scowling frown of disapproval.

Pushing out of his reach, Kaylee slid hurriedly into the seat opposite him, fighting back the urge to wipe away the disturbing effects of his touch. "Alright, Daniel. I'm here. There is no one looking over our shoulder, no one listening in to whatever it is you want to talk to me about. What was so important you needed to meet me here alone to say it?"

"It's not right."

For a minute, she thought he was talking about the way he'd put his hands on her a moment ago and she was about to agree when he said, "I'm back where I started, but it's not the same, Kaylee. Nothing feels *right*. Not without you. *We* are not right."

Uneasy now, she asked, "What do you mean? Daniel, there is no *we*—"

"But there *should* be," he insisted. "We were going to get *married*, Kaylee. Married!"

The way he emphasized the word made her want to cringe. How ironic, she thought. Too bad he couldn't have felt this way four years ago. But none of it mattered. Not now.

"Remember how excited we were? And that dress...beautiful. I'm sorry I never got to see you in it."

Gripping her purse in one hand, she started to stand, but Daniel waved her back.

"I know I did you wrong, sweetheart, and I know you were hurt. I get that. But I can't help but think how good we were together and—I think we should try again, you know? Not immediately. I know you'll need a little time to readjust, but I'm home now and I've apologized, and ... I just want it *back*. I want it *all* back. I want *us* back, what we had before, Kaylee." There was a pleading look in his eyes, one that begged for her to trust the sincerity of his gaze and his tone but, unfortunately for him, it was a look in which she no longer believed.

"Say you'll give me—give *us*—a second chance." Daniel's hand found hers over the table. His fingers squeezed hers and Kaylee's eyes squeezed shut. He must have taken her shocked silence for hesitation because he said, "We had something special, you and I."

"No. No," she finally managed to deny, snatching her fingers from his grasp. "For a long time, I really thought we did. As shameful as it is for me to admit it,when you told me you were mine alone and that you promised to love me forever, I believed you. You really had me fooled, Daniel. So much and so well that when you first left, I thought I might literally die. But that's gone now."

And it really *was* gone, she suddenly realized, and her eyes snapped upward, stunned because it was the truth. She hadn't even noticed the change, but it had happened just the same. In a single instant of revelation, there was no more guilt over thinking she'd been at fault somehow for their breakup, that she hadn't been woman enough to keep him. All the loneliness and grief she'd felt, the months of bitter depression and loneliness, every bit of it and all of the pain simply vanished, disappearing like a thick veil of dark mist that had been whisked away, leaving her almost breathless with relief. It washed over her in waves as the truth of what she had said resonated in her head.

Miraculously, against everything she had believed possible after Daniel had walked out on her four years ago, she realized she was mended— at last. Her bruised and broken heart *had* healed and right then, at that very important moment was when she finally realized she was free. Free from the past. Free to go on with her life. Free to love and be loved. Free to be with Jordan...because she loved him.

Like the fragile glass surrounding the antique snow globe she'd picked up at Seville's the day she and Jordan had met, the delusions she'd suffered under before he came into ·her life had been shattered, and she had Jordan to thank for it. True, she'd once thought Daniel had crushed her, but the truth was he'd only made her shut herself away. But then Jordan had come along, and like a fledgling that relentlessly pecked away at its shell from the inside, he had slipped into her heart and opened up her hardened exterior, freeing her to once again be the warm, loving woman she truly was.

Jordan had released her; he'd made her free to be herself, and the enormity of that, of the gift he had already given her almost took her breath away. Her now steady gaze met Daniel's and held. "Whatever we may have believed we had together before, it wasn't love and it wasn't real. I know that now. I know because this...*this* is different. So very *different*."

She thought about Jordan's text, the clue for the surprise he had for her, and her lips turned up slowly in an ever-widening smile. Whatever it was, it couldn't possibly compare with the beauty and magnitude of emotion flowing inside her right now. She *loved* Jordan! She loved him and she wasn't afraid to admit it. Not anymore.

* * *

Jordan was whistling a catchy tune when he

finally came out of the gift shop where he'd had Kaylee's gift packaged, and wrapped, and then tied with a big frilly bow. It was nestled in a thick pile of finely shredded paper in the bottom of the heavy craft bag he carried but he was still careful not to bump it against anything as he settled it in the seat of his truck on the passenger side. The thing was fragile and he didn't want it to break before she even got to see it.

He could hardly wait to get back to her, to see her face when she opened the package and saw what was inside, but when he rounded the tailgate, he was surprised to see Daniel Sutton leaning casually against the fender of his truck, and he sighed. Why was it that every time he got excited about something problems were wont to crop up everywhere, all determined to cause a delay.

"Sutton," he said, tipping his head slightly in greeting before he opened the door and climbed up into the drivers seat. He would have closed it, too, but Daniel's hand shot out, stopping it in mid-swing.

"Stay away from her, Parker," he demanded, and Jordan's brows rose.

"From whom?"

"Don't play dumb with me, man. You're a genius. I'd say figure it out but we both know you already know who. Stay away from Kaylee. She's mine, got it? Always has been. Always will be."

Jordan could feel his lips curling upward in a derisive smirk. He bit back a chiding laugh. This one wasn't worth it. "Might want to check with

Kaylee about that. I'm pretty sure she has a different opinion on the matter."

The jerk had the gall to cross his arms over his chest without moving out of the way so Jordan could close his door and he smirked back. "She didn't give that impression when we were having coffee together a little while ago."

As he was sure Kaylee's ex had intended, Jordan felt the slicing sting of jealousy rip through him at the thought of her being anywhere near this man again but he tamped it down. If he was ever going to win Kaylee's trust after what Sutton had done to her, he knew he'd have to afford her the benefit of doubt. "You're lying."

"Oh yeah? I asked her about it, actually, how she felt about me and about you. Seems like she's changed her mind, now that I'm home again, and who can blame her? I *was* her first choice, after all." He pulled out a cell phone and held it up to Jordan. "Proof's right there. All you gotta do is hit play."

Jordan took the cell, his piercing gaze casually sliding away from the challenging gleam in Sutton's eyes to the time stamp on the recording. It correlated to just minutes after he'd texted Kaylee about the surprise he was bringing her, but he was so sure Sutton was lying about having had coffee with her, he hit the play button anyway.

Kaylee's soft voice drifted out and Jordan bit back a curse.

"Whatever we may have believed we had together before, it wasn't love and it wasn't real. I know that now.

I know because this...this is different. So very different."

Jordan stiffened. There was something there, something in her tone, in the breathless way she'd said those words that made him uneasy but he would never admit it to this gloating little creep. Sure, he felt wounded she'd had coffee with her ex and hadn't bothered to tell him about it, but that was just male pride. He was also almost positive the bit of conversation Sutton had recorded had a meaning far different from the one he wanted him to believe but just for a moment, uncertainty clouded his reason.

Still, he managed a glare. "Out of context, Sutton. Care to tell me about the rest of Kaylee's side of the conversation, and how she feels about you recording her without her knowing? I'm sure there was more, right? Or was this the best you got?"

Ignoring Jordan's questions, Daniel snatched the phone out of Jordan's hand. "Like I said, stay away from her."

He turned to walk away at the same time Jordan's phone buzzed with a text notification. He flipped it easily out of its case and glanced down at the screen. It was from Kaylee: *Had coffee at Sam's but I'm back at the shelter now. Can't wait to see you – I have a confession to make. Dying to see what you're bringing!*

Doubt reached up and punched him in the gut and he punched it back.

Fine, he thought. So Sutton hadn't been lying about having coffee with her. Sam's was a public coffee shop and he was sure Kaylee had a good reason for meeting him there, but ... why hadn't she mentioned anything about it to him—either today or last night?

Chapter Twenty

Driving past the shelter without stopping was one of the hardest things Jordan had done lately, but he needed to think without distraction and Kaylee was the one distraction he wasn't yet prepared to face. Granted, she was a good kind of distraction, but right now the doubt churning in his gut was making him crazy. If he were to stop, to pick her up now, he knew he'd be a total grouch.

The last thing he wanted to do was accuse her of something she hadn't said, or done, or even felt, but uncertainty was riding him hard after his unexpected meet-up with Sutton and he had to be sure he was prepared to deal with seeing her, being with her, to hearing her answers to his questions—no matter what they might be—before he saw her again. If she'd decided to reconcile with Daniel ...

Less than fifteen minutes later, not even bothering to wait for the doors on the garage to open so he could drive inside, Jordan pulled into his driveway and killed the engine on his truck. Grabbing the package from the passenger seat, he hopped out, whistled for Sarge, and went up the walk to the front of the house instead of going in through the side door, as had become his habit. He'd barely made it inside when his cell phone signaled he'd received a text from Kaylee: *Was that you I saw drive past about fifteen minutes ago?*

Ignoring her text for the moment, he went through to set the surprise he'd picked up for Kaylee on his kitchen table, then came back to close and lock his front door before he stopped in the middle of the living room and just stood there, staring down at his phone again. He should answer her, but if he replied back *yes*, she was going to want to know why he hadn't stopped and he didn't think he could tell her. Not yet. He wasn't even sure of the reason himself.

No, that wasn't true. He *was* sure. He'd found out she'd spent time over coffee with her ex and jealousy was gnawing at him, along with doubt and not a little bit of fear. The question he had ignored earlier came back to annoy him. What if she had decided to reconcile with Daniel? Was this the reason for her no strings policy—she'd been hoping Daniel would come back all along? Had she held out with him in hopes she and Daniel could be together again?

He realized all he had to do was ask her. She would tell him the truth—even if he didn't like what she had to say. It was mustering the courage to ask that had him wavering over whether or not to answer her text. Finally, he slid his thumb across the face of his phone to wake it and texted back: *Yes. Had something to do first.*

He didn't bother to add that thinking about her, about them, and why he was no longer content to leave things as they were was the something he'd desperately needed to do before he could see her again. She didn't reply right away, so he put his phone down on the coffee table beside one of the antique letter boxes she'd recently filled. This one had become his new remote control caddy, and the one on the little round table by the stairs was for his pocket stuffs. She'd pointed out how perfectly placed it was—he could empty his pockets before he went upstairs for bed and return whatever he needed the following morning when he came back down.

Looking around at all the boxes now placed in strategic locations around his house, he finally realized why he'd been so obsessed with buying the things in the first place. They were symbolic of himself, of how he'd felt for so long now it was almost second nature. Nice on the outside but on the inside? Empty.

Like him, most of the boxes showed outward signs of wear but each one was still warm and genuine and beautiful, he supposed, in its own way. Outside, there were definite signs of life. But there had been nothing on the inside—of the boxes or his heart—until the day he'd bought the box with the dog tag inside which had led him to Kaylee.

That was the day everything changed.

He had changed. Instead of a soul looking for a box to fill, his heart had became a box in want of filling ... and Kaylee had done it. She had come into his life and slowly filled his heart the same way she had filled the empty boxes—with caring, with surprising insight into his soul, with sweetly endearing, unforgettable little bits of herself—one piece at a time, until the boxes, his heart, his home —everything he possessed—was filled with love.

Turning, he glanced at the bag on his table and thought of the antique box and the surprise carefully cradled inside—the one he had picked up at Seville's. This one, he had altered. He'd done it with Kaylee in mind, out of his love for her— though he hadn't realized it at the time, and he'd done it because he wanted to make her happy.

Finally, he understood that was what he'd wanted for a long time—ever since he'd first seen her that day outside Seville's. He wanted to make her happy because he loved her. He had believed she was coming to care for him, too. Wasn't that what she had meant when she'd told him the place for new beginnings was in their hearts? But then Daniel had showed up, and ... Scooping up his phone, he swiped it with his thumb and started typing.

* * *

Half an hour later, Jordan led her through his living room and into the kitchen. He hadn't said why he'd come home before picking her up at the shelter. In fact, he hadn't said much of anything on the ride over—only that she could make her confession later, that they both needed to talk, but he wanted to give her her surprise first. He refused to give her another hint about what it was, too, no matter how many times she asked—and she had asked more than once.

"Can I peek now?" she asked, but she didn't dare move her hands for fear of ruining the surprise before he was ready.

"No, not yet. I have to open the bag. Keep your eyes closed, Kaylee Dean. No peeking!"

"But I've been waiting all day to see what you got! You know I have no patience when it comes to things like this," she said, her eyes still closed and dutifully covered with both hands.

When he finally allowed her to lower her hands, Kaylee was stunned to see the letter box he had bought at Seville's sitting open on the table. It would never close again, for inside sat a replica of the snow-globe she had purchased that same day.

"I know you said the snow globe was nothing special, that it shouldn't mean anything to you because you hadn't had it long, and yet you were in tears when it shattered. I took a chance that you just hadn't figured out your attachment yet." He shrugged. "The interior bits are a little different in this one but it's got the same house and trees and the scene is mostly the same. I hope that's okay?"

"Oh, Jordan, it's beautiful!" Her hands slid lovingly over the new glass globe, over the letter box he'd bought the day they'd met outside the antique shop that now served as a base, and she shook her head to help fight back the tears that threatened. "It wasn't the scene inside that drew me, anyway. Not really. It was more what I felt, what I thought I could believe in, whenever I looked inside."

"Oh? And what was that? Come on, you can tell me," he teased with a friendly nudge to the shoulder. "We're friends, remember?"

Glancing up at him, she said, "It was the same thing I felt every time I saw or heard or thought of *you—*"

Her voice cracked and she looked away, focusing on the globe rather than the way his eyes darkened at her words. She didn't have the words to explain. How could she tell him the snow globe had come to represent everything Daniel's defection had denied her? How could she make him understand when she looked in the globe, the fragile glass surrounding her heart hadn't felt quite so confining anymore?

Somehow, it had made her feel as if it were okay to dream again, to trust, to believe in love, in the possibility and promise of a happily ever after—for her, and so she had. Thanks to him. Like the fragile glass surrounding the scene inside the snow globe, all the fire, passion, and love inside her heart had been encased with fear of being hurt again—until Jordan had come along and shattered the hardened exterior, freeing her to be herself again, to be the warm, loving woman she truly was.

"What did you feel, Kaylee?" His words were low, rough.

She felt the gentle nudge of his finger beneath

her chin and glanced up into his eyes, fighting the sting of tears that wanted to cloud her own. She even tried to smile but it came out all wobbly and she had to suck in a breath to keep from bursting into tears. Finally, she managed to get the words out around the thick lump of emotion swelling in her throat. "Something magical."

She felt his fingers slide into her hair an instant before his lips touched hers. Her breath escaping on a contented sigh, she rose up on her tip-toes to better fit her lips to his while her arms slid around his waist, but she barely noticed anything beyond how perfect it felt to be held by him.

Kissing Jordan just felt right. When she was in his arms, the world and all its problems fell away, leaving only the two of them and a sense of contentment she'd never experienced before. It felt so wonderful she never wanted to step away from his embrace.

But then, he broke the kiss and the confusion, the questions she saw in his eyes when she opened hers brought her crashing down to earth real fast. "Jordan?"

Stepping away, he let his fingers twine with hers. He cleared his throat. "This would probably be a good time for me to hear your confession."

Her confession? She remembered her text and could immediately feel the blush coloring her cheeks. "Oh, that."

Jordan tilted his head, giving her a quizzical look. "Yes, that. Does it have anything to do with your ex?"

Kaylee frowned. "Not really, but why would you ask that?"

Jordan let go of her hands and folded his arms over his chest. "Because he cornered me in a parking lot in Center this afternoon to give me a message. He even played a bit of a conversation between the two of you he said he recorded while you and he shared a coffee today at Sam's."

Kaylee's brow rose. "We had *separate* coffees and … a message? What message?"

"It was more a warning, really. To stay away from you. He says you chose him first and now you want him back. Is that true, Kaylee? Do you want to be with Daniel again?"

"What? No! Why would I want … wait a minute. You said he *recorded* our conversation? Well, if he played back to you what I actually said to him you already know I would never—" She broke off. "He didn't record everything I said. He played a selective bit of our conversation and … you believed him, didn't you? You believed I wanted him back."

Jordan leaned back, his hip propped against the edge of the table. "I didn't want to, Kaylee. I didn't believe you would meet him without mentioning it to me, either, but you did, and it *was* your voice I heard on his cell phone, saying things like 'It wasn't love before' and 'This is so different'.

Crossing his arms over his chest, he scowled at her in confusion. "Damn it, Kaylee, I see that accusing look creeping into your eyes, and I don't like this any more than you apparently do, but what was I supposed to think?"

"That I was telling him what I felt for him in the past wasn't what I thought it was? And that I was explaining the reason I knew it wasn't what he'd believed it to be was because of how different I feel when I'm with *you*?"

Kaylee could feel her anger rising in reaction to his lack of trust and she suddenly felt like lashing out. "But you and I, we are just *friends*, right? And as my *friend*, you should have been happy for me. You should—"

"I *love* you, Kaylee."

In shock at his bluntly stated announcement, her eyes whipped up to meet his. He didn't move. His expression didn't change one tiny bit, not even when he repeated the words.

"I love you. And when I hear from that creep that you've spent time with him, I find myself in an awkward position—one where I just want to break things—and I hate it. I don't like what knowing you've been with him—even for something as innocent as coffee—makes me feel inside, in here," he said, slamming his palm against his chest. "And I don't ever want to experience it again."

She looked away, hesitant and uncertain whether or not she should believe him.

"That was to be my confession, you know?"she said finally, her tone wry. "Not that I had coffee with Daniel today, but the other. I didn't even realize it until I was sitting at that table with him, wishing I was with *you* the entire time. But it was there that I finally understood, finally realized why it didn't bother me that he'd come back. Why I wasn't wracked with torturous indecision and why I didn't feel the pain of our breakup the way I had before."

Jordan peered at her. "Wait. I think I missed something. What, exactly, did you realize?"

"How much I love you, Jordan H. Parker, retired billionaire ex-IT guy," she said, and her smile practically lit up the room. She walked over and leaned against him, sliding her hands up his chest to his shoulders. "I love you, and knowing how wonderful *this* feels, the way I feel for you, I'm almost ashamed to admit that I don't think I ever really loved Daniel at all. Well, not as anything more than a friend."

"In that case ..." He bent and scooped her up into his arms before heading to the stairs.

"Jordan, wait!" she squealed. "What are you doing?"

"Taking you upstairs, Kaylee. I find I cannot wait another minute to make you ... *feel things.*"

"Oh?" she asked, looping her fingers at the back of his neck, a teasing smile flirting across her lips now that she was certain of his feelings for her. "And just what do you propose to make me feel, Mr. Parker?"

He took the stairs two at a time in his haste, and as he carried her up the wide staircase, Kaylee's gaze drifted back to the antique letter box standing open on his kitchen table, now serving as the perfect base for her newly repaired snow globe. *How like Jordan and I those two are,* she thought.

Apart, much like she and Jordan had been, they were empty and broken and alone. But together they each had purpose. Together, they were filled and fulfilled and whole.

"Something magical," he said, his voice was low and husky with promise—one that matched the look in his eyes—as he pushed open the door to his bedroom and then carried her inside where he deposited her carefully on his bed. It was the promise of forever.

ABOUT THE AUTHOR

USA Today bestselling author, Leighann Dobbs, discovered her passion for writing after a twenty year career as a software engineer. She lives in New Hampshire with her husband Bruce, their trusty Chihuahua mix Mojo and beautiful rescue cat, Kitty. Her book "Dead Wrong" won the "Best Mystery Romance" award at the 2014 Indie Romance Convention. Her book "Ghostly Paws" was the 2015 Chanticleer Mystery & Mayhem First Place category winner in the Animal Mystery category. When she's not reading, gardening, making jewelry or selling antiques, she likes to write cozy mystery and historical romance books.

Sneak Peek!

Enjoy a look inside Chapter 1 of Book 2 in the Witches of Hawthorne Grove series...

Samuel Ethan Huntingdon III stood in the middle of his mostly bare, eleven hundred and some odd square feet of workshop, both hands stuffed in the pockets of his worn jeans, while he watched his newly engaged best friend, Jordan Parker, carefully disassemble the antique *chiffonier* he'd purchased at an estate sale a while back.

"You're going to need to replace some of the hardware." Jordan handed him the door and then the hardware—a pair of ruined iron hinges and what was left of a once intricately crafted wooden pull handle—he'd just removed. "You might be able to find these at Seville's. If not, I can check with a few people in Center, but I'd stop in at Seville's first."

Seville's was actually *Seville's Antiques and Collectibles*—a battered, run-down, miserable looking little shop on the edge of town that just happened to be the only genuine antique store in Hawthorne Grove. The place was managed by three sisters who'd lived in the area since way before Sam moved into the small town a handful years ago. Jordan had found an antique letter box there shortly after he'd come to Hawthorne Grove—one he claimed was instrumental in getting him an introduction to his soon to be wife—and Kaylee Dean, his fiance, said the same thing about a snow globe she'd purchased there.

"Great idea. Maybe I'll run into my future wife while I'm there and we can get started building a replica antique cradle when we finish with the restoration of this old thing," Sam teased.

"Go ahead and laugh, old man. Your turn's coming." Jordan shot back. His reply was muffled because he was leaning head and shoulders inside the cabinet, thumping and fumbling around with something inside. Shelves, most likely, Sam thought, until the door swung back and Jordan emerged, holding what looked like an old quilt rack—at least that's what he thought they were. It was what his Grandmother had always called the things she kept near the foot of every bed in her house, anyway.

This one was a little bit plain. It bare and dusty and a little beat up, but with some wax and polish and some simple good old TLC, Sam knew it would be as good as new. He reached out to take it so he could set it aside for now, but Jordan was too busy inspecting the thing to hand it over.

"What in the world? Looks like a hand-made saw horse or something," Jordan said, eyeing the piece quizzically. "No, I don't think so, now that I give it a closer look. It's too detailed for that but I don't think I've seen anything like it before. You got any ideas, Sammy?"

"It's a quilt rack," he said, proud to be able to claim a little knowledge—in this area, at least. "Gramma used to have one of these in every bedroom."

Each one had always seemed to be holding a different variety of hand-sewn quilts, too, as he recalled, all lovingly stitched by his grandmother and sometimes, a few of her friends. The smell of springtime and sunshine seemed to have been infused into them, too, now that he thought about it.

Gramma never had embraced the idea of electric dryers. She hung her quilts outdoors on the clothesline Grampa had stretched for her until the day she'd died, and the scent of her quilts, freshly taken in off the line, was one Sam didn't think he'd ever forget. She'd been snuggling him into the things since he was a toddler.

Shaking free of the unexpected wave of nostalgia, he glanced up and caught Jordan still eyeing the thing skeptically. He tried to explain. "A quilt rack, Jordan. You know? A place where you store your extra quilts when they're not being used every night but it's still too cool out to stuff them away into the back of the linen closet for summer storage?"

He reached over to take the piece from his friend and set it to one side. "I remember coming in late, sneaking up the back stairs back before

Gramma passed away. She would catch me every time. She'd give me a pat, feel my cheeks, worry over how chilled I was, and tell me there were plenty of extra quilts by the bed if I needed them. All I had to do was pick one and snuggle in."

"Gramma Ellie." Jordan nodded. "She was a great lady, Sam. I know you miss her."

Sam nodded. "She and Grampa were the only constants in my life. Dad was always out in his rig on yet another cross-country run, but the only running Gramma ever did was to the grocery store on Wednesdays. Remember that? I used to think the only reason she went there was to pick up cookies. "

Jordan sat the quilt rack to one side and leaned one hip against the wardrobe, a smile of fond reminiscence on his lips. He chuckled. "Double fudge chocolate chip. How could I forget?"

"Did Sam forget Lindsey's coming by the coffee shop today, or have you two decided to play in here all day?" Kaylee Dean, Jordan's fiance, poked her head around the workshop door to ask. Lindsey Vale, the owner of Vale Vintage Interiors and a long-time friend of Kaylee's older sister, was coming in to talk with him about upgrading the coffee shop.

Jordan handed over the hardware he'd removed from the *chiffonier* and hurried across the shop to greet her with a warm kiss while Sam looked wryly on. "We were just about to head out, Kaylee. Now that you're here, you can help us wrangle Sarge out of Sammy's forty acre field out back."

The field in question was really just a huge back yard Sam had recently fenced in where his new Husky pup, Jabez, was allowed to roam free. Kaylee laughed. "Sarge loves it when you bring him for a visit now. I think he likes playing protector."

It only took a minute to collect the Golden Retriever Jordan had adopted from the animal shelter where Kaylee worked a few months ago from his back yard, and then Sam walked with them to Jordan's pick-up.

"I'll meet you two at the coffee shop," he promised Kaylee. "Jordan says I should stop by Seville's to look for replacement hardware and since it's on the way, I think I'll stop in. If the sisters don't have what I need, you can ask around in Center this afternoon when you and Kaylee go up to look at wedding dresses."

* * *

The soft sound of musical bells ringing over the door of the antique shop was accompanied by an almost electrical hum of awareness that brought Emma Riley's head springing up, but only long enough for her to peek inquisitively through her lashes and over the rim of her glasses to see who had come inside.

A tallish man with hair the color of wet sand and a contagious friendly smile walked into the showroom, surprise clearly evident on his face at how different the interior of the small antique shop was in comparison with the almost frighteningly debilitated look of the exterior.

Hiding a smile, she quickly ducked her head back down before he could make eye contact, forcing herself to focus once again on the display of antique puzzle boxes in front of her instead of checking him out.

As a Freelance Research Specialist, her job often brought her into contact with all sorts of rare, artful things, but her latest client, a writer, needed some information about antique puzzles and that was why she had driven down here this morning— to see what she could find, if anything.

Her friend, Lindsey Vale, had suggested this particular shop. Lindsey was an interior decorator and she frequently hung out in antique shops or at estate sales, looking for the perfect pieces with which to transform the bland, boring interiors of her clientele. Lindsey had warned her about the fallacy of Seville's battered exterior, promising sheer magic awaiting her beyond the ramshackle appearance and half-rotted wooden doors.

Emma hadn't been so certain when she'd gotten her first look at the place. Once inside, however, she'd found herself enchanted by the beautiful selections on offer and now was having a difficult time making up her mind over which of the puzzles waiting with infinite patience in front of her that she should buy. She hadn't actually come in this morning with the intent to actually purchase a puzzle, but now that she was here, looking directly at them instead of viewing them from a set of badly shot photographs on the

Internet, she couldn't seem to will herself to resist.

One puzzle in particular, made from an especially warm hardwood with a slightly worn image of a charming Victorian couple on front, pulled at her. She knew she'd probably settle on it in the end, but right now, she was enjoying the momentary back and forth debate in her mind of trying to decide between it and another which sported an ancient world map—which she loved—but it seemed far less sophisticated as far as the cut of the individual pieces went.

"Good morning! Can we help you, sir?" came the lilting voice of the woman who had settled behind the counter a few moments before, right after she'd carefully lain out the most interesting quilt Emma had ever seen.

Made up of black and white squares, each one sewn together in a lovely pattern she knew probably had a name though she hadn't a clue what it might be, Emma figured the only reason she found the antique coverlet intriguing was because it was so simple. The piece was crisp. Practical. Useful. A bit like herself, she supposed. Maybe that was why the thing kept drawing her eye?

"It is lovely, isn't it?" The woman behind the counter ran her hand over the material in a gentle sweep, caressing the fabric as if it were something precious and rare. "The lady we acquired it from said it had been in her family for at least six generations, and look—not a stitch out of place after all that time."

"My grandmother made one like this, only she used bits of multicolored fabric where this one has solids. Interesting that this piece was done in simple black and white," the man who had come in earlier replied, his voice moved over her slowly, and like a ray of sunshine stepping boldly out from behind the shadows of a cloud, it warmed her.

Blushing at the realization, Emma cast a quick, surreptitious gaze in his direction, and gasped. She had somehow managed to gravitate over to the counter without the slightest awareness of having done so, and she was now standing right beside him—so close she could feel the heat emanating from his body! No wonder she had imagined his voice was warming her like the sun!

Flustered now, she glanced down at the quilt they'd been discussing. The sight of his large, tanned hand resting firmly atop the cloth conjured imaginings of that same hand on her body, smoothing gently across the tense muscles of her shoulders and back, and her gaze jerked upward once more. It clashed with his and held, refusing to break away.

"The simplicity of it is what makes it so special," Emma said, responding in a voice gone breathless, and to her surprise, he wholeheartedly agreed.

"I'll take it," he said, glancing up at the proprietress, "along with four sets of each of these if you have them." He held out his other hand to show the woman what he needed, and Emma, now freed from the intensity of his gaze, was suddenly galvanized into action.

"Oh, no. You can't! It's—" Emma laid the puzzle box she didn't remember picking up on the counter beside the quilt and turned an imploring gaze on the woman behind it, her fingers finding and sliding over the warm cloth. "I—I'd already decided to purchase it, you see," she fibbed, stuttering out an explanation while her eyes silently willed the shopkeeper to go along before she said, "I'll take the puzzle, too."

Guilt over her fib instantly plaguing her, Emma tilted her head upward by tiny degrees until her eyes met his—and she could feel the cloth beneath her fingertips changing, firming, expanding until it seemed to have come alive and now felt as if she were caressing the planes and contours of familiar bare skin—sculpted, muscular, hot *male* skin.

Her body was spontaneously delighted while her fingers tingled with pleasure, similarly thrilled at the touch. Gasping, Emma snatched her hand away and quickly turned her head away to break eye contact with the handsome stranger, but not before she noticed the flecks of tawny gold highlighting his eyes go bright, changing the bright green to a marbled, molten amber.

Flushed with embarrassment, her face heated. He couldn't possibly have known what she was thinking. Could he? Keeping her gaze lowered, she merely nodded her head when the woman behind the counter asked if she wanted the puzzle and quilt wrapped. She could sense movement at her side, but didn't dare look up again. Not while he was still there.

The minute the puzzle and quilt were both wrapped and bagged, Emma hastily signed her name on the check she'd been making out and handed it to the woman, then grabbed up both packages and hurried from the store, head down, her eyes firmly focused on nothing but the path in front of her.

OTHER BOOKS BY LEIGHANN DOBBS

Contemporary Romance

***

Reluctant Romance

Some Like It Hot

————

Regency Romance

***

The Unexpected Series:

An Unexpected Proposal

Dobbs Fancytales

Regency Fairytales:

The Beast of Edenmaine

The Reluctant Princess

Something in Red

Dancing on Glass

Snow White and the Seven Rogues

Sleeping Heiress

Dobbs Fancytales Boxed Set Collection

(includes all six short stories)

Western Historical Romance

***

Goldwater Creek Mail Order Brides:
Faith

American Mail Order Brides Series:
Chevonne: Bride of Oklahoma

———

COZY MYSTERIES

Mystic Notch
Cat Cozy Mystery Series

* * *

Ghostly Paws
A Spirited Tail
A Mew To A Kill
Paws and Effect

———

Blackmoore Sisters
Cozy Mystery Series

* * *

Dead Wrong
Dead & Buried

Dead Tide

Buried Secrets

Deadly Intentions

A Grave Mistake

Spell Found

Mooseamuck Island

Cozy Mystery Series

* * *

A Zen For Murder

A Crabby Killer

A Treacherous Treasure

Lexy Baker

Cozy Mystery Series

* * *

Lexy Baker Cozy Mystery Series Boxed Set Vol 1

(Books 1-4)

Or buy the books separately:

Killer Cupcakes

Dying For Danish

Murder, Money and Marzipan

3 Bodies and a Biscotti

Brownies, Bodies & Bad Guys

Bake, Battle & Roll

Wedded Blintz

Scones, Skulls & Scams

Ice Cream Murder

Mummified Meringues

Brutal Brulee (Novella)